13895

D0209619

A HYMN IS BORN

A HYMN IS BORN

Clint Bonner

Illustrated by CHARLES E. SMITH

BROADMAN PRESS
Nashville, Tennessee

Library of Congress card catalog number 59–9694
Printed in the United States of America

Dedication

To two noble souls who taught me to love
the hymns of the church—my mother and
my father—the latter being

A PREACHER I KNEW

There are men who toil to build a name,
Who squander life for wealth and fame.
I knew a man who had no gold,
Whose treasure was a brother's soul.

For three score years and more than ten
He lived his life for other men,
In modest church and humble home
With scarce a day to call his own.

No choir in robes behind him sang;
No chime in roof above him rang;
He said no lines that men prepare,
But from his heart he read his prayer.

The hymns he sang were those I know—
The ones he taught me years ago—
"On Jordan's Stormy Banks I Stand"
And "Hold to God's Unchanging Hand."

Beside the tomb where teardrops start
He gently soothed a broken heart;
And children gathered at his knee
To hear him tell of Galilee.

A thousand souls were waiting there,
The day he went their joy to share;
A thousand souls he showed the way
To life and love and endless day.

Introduction

When a journalist takes the colorful stories of hymn history out of the scholar's study and returns these to the general public, that is news in itself. But when he does so in such a readable way as Clint Bonner has done in this attractive book, this is indeed something!

A look at the inviting table of contents quickly gives one the flavor of this book: "A Baby Girl Is Born to a Yankee Carpenter," "A Composer Dodges Traffic and Writes a Melody," "A Bank Clerk and a Shoe Clerk Stop for a Chat." Each of the hymns and tunes treated in this book is given a short, readable, vignette treatment that should win a warm welcome from all the family.

I am particularly conscious of hymn history as I write these words because I am seated at the little desk at which my ancestor Thomas Hastings wrote his familiar tune for Toplady's "Rock of Ages."

When we sing hymns, most of us seldom think how far back in history hymn singing really goes. We forget how often in the Old Testament we read accounts of the Israelites' singing songs of praise. When we read from the book of Psalms, actually we are reading from a hymnbook. Similarly, in the New Testament we read of the angels that first Christmas singing their "glory to God in the highest" and of Jesus and his disciples singing a hymn in the upper room after the Last Supper. When Paul and Silas were cast into prison, what did they do? The New Testament tells us that they sang hymns! One can just imagine one jailer saying to another, "Those Christians—you've got to admit it; they *have* something." Yes, our hymn history goes back many centuries.

In this book Clint Bonner tells the stories behind hymns and hymn tunes from many churches, many centuries, many lands. As we read these brief accounts of old favorites and learn about some which are less familiar, we perhaps come to realize anew that hymns are indeed a "tie that binds," for hymns have a unique way of bringing together people of many communions. Side by side in standard hymnals are the works, for example, of Unitarians, Roman Catholics, Episcopalians, and Presbyterians—all of us. When we sing "Onward Christian Soldiers," we sing the words, "We are not divided, all one body we." Probably these words are never truer of denominationally divided Christians than when we are singing hymns.

Hymns do not belong just in the choir loft but to all the people everywhere. Hymns belong not just in church services but at school and at home as well. I have long been a great believer in the value of hymn singing as the least self-conscious way to begin family worship. For whether it be for grace at meals, prayers at bedtime, or informal singing around the living room piano, hymn singing can be both fun and a deepening spiritual experience.

With this book, you and your family can make friends with the stories behind many hymns and tunes. Think how much more those hymns will mean for your having learned their origins!

With this book, you and your family can play "Did you know?" games based on the hymn stories. For example, "What hymn is believed to have been written in only fifteen minutes?" "What hymn was taken from the dictionary?" "What hymn writer wrote sixty-five hundred hymns?"

With this book, you can read the stories of hymns and then use the hymns themselves as a part of your own private devotions. Who knows? You might even be inspired to write a text or tune of your own!

In any case, chances are that this friendly book will win a warm welcome in your home. Some of the hymns, you may say, are better than others. That is no doubt quite true. But as Evelyn Underhill once reminded us, "The silliest hymn and most formal prayer can be made a great act of worship if those who use it have worshiping instead of critical hearts."

LEE HASTINGS BRISTOL, JR.

Preface

It has been said that man has crowded more material progress into the first half of the twentieth century than in all the thousands of years of previous recorded history. But regardless of man's progress in things material, some things he cannot improve upon. For some things are eternal—as fixed as the stars. And it is only through deeper understanding and appreciation of these things eternal that man can fully benefit from them.

Religion is eternal. And the time-honored hymns of our churches are a fixed part of religious worship. "Then sang Moses and the children of Israel this song unto the Lord" (Ex. 15:1). "All the congregation worshipped, and the singers sang" (2 Chron. 29:28). "All the earth shall worship thee, and shall sing unto thee; they shall sing to thy name" (Psalm 66:4). These are but a few of many biblical references to singing in worship.

Christian hymns are as old as the Christian religion—as old as the New Testament. And, of course, the Psalms were sung centuries before Christ. In Christian churches, however, congregational singing was frowned upon for fifteen centuries after Christ, and for any but the clergy to sing was looked upon as heresy and was punishable by imprisonment. It was not until after Martin Luther broke from the Roman Catholic Church and championed the Reformation that congregational singing came into general practice. Even two centuries after Luther the singing of any but the Psalms of David was regarded by some denominations as sacrilegious. Hymns of "human composure" were frowned upon as "scandalous doggerel."

During the early 1500's Martin Luther wrote thirty-seven hymns for his "Protestants" to sing. Because of ancient opposition to congregational singing and the unpopularity of singing any but the songs of David in many churches, few writers dared add to Luther's efforts. But in the seventeenth century the man and the hour met.

England's infirm little literary genius, Isaac Watts, boldly set about to "Christianize" a selection of Psalms by paraphrasing them. Watts published his "modernized" Psalms in a book entitled *Psalms of David Imitated,* and English hymns as we know them today were born. Frail, dwarfish, ingenious Isaac Watts dared to depart from an ancient custom. Where others before him had timidly failed, Watts blazed the way for August Toplady, Charles Wesley, John Newton, William Cowper, and many others.

In the broad sense, all songs of worship might be called hymns. Yet in a more strict sense Christian songs fall into three general categories—hymns, gospel hymns, and gospel songs. If this seems confusing, the reader might make a few random comparisons. In the class of the stately, scholarly hymn are such titles as "Rock of Ages," "Lead, Kindly Light," and "Jesus, Lover of My Soul." Compare these, words and music, with the lighter gospel song, such as "Life's Railway to Heaven," "There Shall be Showers of Blessing," and "Brighten the Corner Where You Are." Between these two extremes falls the gospel hymn. It is not quite up to literary standards of the scholarly hymn; yet it is of higher quality than the usual gospel song. Typical of the gospel hymn are "Rescue the Perishing," "Near the Cross," and "Safe in the Arms of Jesus."

In the broad sense, the eighteenth century was the era of the scholarly hymn. Beginning with Isaac Watts, this was the era of Charles Wesley, William Cowper, John Newton, August Toplady, Samuel Stennett, and others, from whose pens came such hymns as "Majestic Sweetness Sits Enthroned," "How Firm a Foundation," "O for a Thousand Tongues to Sing," and "Rock of Ages."

The half century following 1825 is usually referred to as the "Mason Era." This was the period of Lowell Mason, the dedicated composer who did more, perhaps, than any other American to encourage interest in church singing. During this period were written such favorites as "Nearer, My God, to Thee," "Just As I Am," and "Sweet Hour of Prayer." During the 1850's—the period of Stephen Foster's lilting secular melodies—there came a lighter trend in religious songs, the gospel hymn. These were followed, during the great revival campaigns of the last century, by the still lighter gospel song. Neither of these types measures up to literary standards of the stately hymn. As a rule, they differ also in that instead of being directed to God, they express personal hope and sentiment.

Of Isaac Watts' 650 hymns, perhaps no more than twenty survive in current use. Of Charles Wesley's six thousand titles, a safe estimate of surviving numbers might be set at thirty. Of Fanny Crosby's nine thousand gospel hymns, some thirty-five promise to live through the ages. Hence it becomes obvious that our present hymnals comprise the best selections from scores of writers and tens of thousands of Christian songs—hymns, gospel hymns, and gospel songs.

As a rule, hymns know no denomination. It would be highly impractical to attempt a selection of strictly Baptist hymns, Methodist hymns, Presbyterian hymns, or hymns exclusive to any one denomination. For Presbyterian hymnals contain titles of the Baptists and the Methodists. The Methodists sing Baptist favorites. Baptist hymnbooks contain titles favored by Methodists, and so on.

The authors are similarly intermixed. Hardly a Protestant hymnal fails to include Roman Catholic Cardinal John Henry Newman's "Lead, Kindly Light." And Father Frederick W. Faber's 150 hymns are well represented in Protestant hymnals, notably by "Faith of Our Fathers." "Silent Night, Holy Night" also is from the pen of a Roman Catholic priest.

The author of "Christ Arose" was a Baptist minister. A Presbyterian minister wrote "Rise Up, O Men of God." "I Love to Tell the Story" is from the pen of an Anglican. "Jesus, Lover of My Soul" was written by a Methodist; "Rock of Ages" by a Calvinist. "All Hail the Power of Jesus' Name" was written by an independent.

A selection of gospel hymns and gospel songs has been included in this book along with the more stately hymns. I have attempted no evaluation of hymn-poems on their merits as literature. That is willingly left to those more qualified. For to me—whether in hymns, gospel hymns or gospel songs—the authors represented in this collection had one common purpose: to make his contribution to Christian worship in song. And not one has done a job lacking in admiration.

Each of the stories in this collection has been written so as to stand separate and independent of any other. Therefore, should the reader be interested in a particular hymn story, he should not feel the necessity of referring to any other story.

As nearly as is feasible I have sought to arrange the stories in chronological order—the oldest hymn represented being presented first, and so on to those most recently written. By this arrangement the reader will gain some knowledge of the evolution of hymn writing. But this arrangement is only general; for I have, at the same time, grouped the selections by individual authors. And during the productive period of an author, his contemporaries are also to be dealt with.

Collection of data upon which to base the following stories has necessitated a wide variety of sources. In addition to available works on the subject, encyclopedias, history books, and biographies have been extensively used. Over the period of two decades required to complete this collection, considerable correspondence and travel have also been necessary. The sources have been so diversified that the listing of a bibliography would have, in itself, added tremendously to the task. Therefore, being a work intended primarily for the layman, and not having been prepared expressly for the student, reference notes and bibliographical listings are omitted.

In addition to many others who have been helpful in the preparation of this work, I am deeply grateful to Gordon and Herbert Shorney, of the Hope Publishing Company, Chicago, for aid in research and for permission to reprint a title under their copyright; to John D. Raridan, executive editor of the Brush-Moore Newspapers, Canton, Ohio, for source material on Will Thompson; to Rev. James C. Moore, Sr., Abbeyville, Georgia, for source material and permission to reprint "Where We'll Never Grow Old"; to Dr. William Pierson Merrill, New York City, for source material and permission to reprint "Rise Up, O Men of God"; to W. B. Walbert, of the James D. Vaughan Publishing Company, Lawrenceburg, Tennessee, for invaluable co-operation; and to my brother, Francis W. Bonner, Ph.D., for his painstaking care in proofreading.

It is hoped that these stories might serve the purpose for which they were written—to encourage a deeper appreciation of the grand old hymns of the church. If that should be accomplished, even to a small degree, the time and effort put into the preparation of this collection will have been well spent. So with my humble thanks to God for permitting the completion of this modest contribution, this work is reverently sent on its way as a tribute to the memory of those noble souls who each made a far greater contribution—the authors and composers of these immortal hymns.

Contents

xv

1. The Oldest Known Christian Hymn

How old is hymn singing? Who wrote the first hymn? One might as well ask, "How old is music?" "Who wrote the first note?"

Because George Washington did so much for his country, he is regarded as its first president. Actually, Washington was fifth. His four predecessors, under the Articles of Confederation—John Hanson, Elias Boudinot, John Hancock, and Nathaniel Gorham—are seldom mentioned.

Because Robert Fulton did so much toward the development of the steamship, he is regarded as its inventor. Mention is rarely made of Barcelona's Blasco de Garay and his steamboat of 1543, or of James Rumey's steam-propelled boat of 1783, or of John Fitch and his steamboat of 1786—all predecessors of Fulton.

So it is with hymn writing. Because Isaac Watts wrote 650 hymns at a time when departure from the ancient custom of Psalm singing was regarded as heresy, the little Englishman has gone down in church annals as the father of the English hymn. Actually, there were many other hymn writers in England and other parts of Europe long before Watts.

Three centuries before Watts, Martin Luther wrote thirty-seven hymns. His "Away in a Manger" and "A Mighty Fortress Is Our God" are still heard around the world.

St. Francis of Assisi wrote "All Creatures of Our God and King" one sweltering summer day in 1225. Theodulph of Orleans penned "All Glory, Laud, and Honor" while in prison in 821. And Bishop Ambrose of Milan wrote "Splendor of God's Glory Bright" during the latter part of the fourth century.

The oldest hymn found in today's hymnbooks was translated from

1

a poem in a book of philosophy, *The Instructor,* written about A.D. 200 by the Greek librarian, preacher, and teacher, Titus Flavius Clemens, usually known as Clement of Alexandria.

The hymn has undergone so many translations that Clement would hardly recognize it in its present form. In popularity it is far down the list. It is given here only because of its distinction as being the oldest known Christian hymn—seventeen and a half centuries old.

> Shepherd of tender youth,
> Guiding in love and truth,
>   Through devious ways;
> Christ our triumphant King,
> We come Thy name to sing,
> Hither our children bring
>   To shout Thy praise.

2. A Catholic Priest Defies the Pope

Mild-mannered John Huss dared differ with the ancient Roman Church. Among other things, he said men should commune directly with God. He said that singing in church should not be restricted to the clergy. For this and other speeches of heresy the gentle Bohemian paid with his life at the stake in 1415. But the ashes of John Huss had hardly cooled when his followers launched a war of revenge. Blood flowed almost unceasingly for fourteen years. Such were religious conditions in Europe five and a half centuries ago.

A century after John Huss was burned to death a German peasant named Martin Luther was working his way through school when he came near being killed by a bolt of lightning. Pondering his close call with death, Luther changed his course of study from law to that of theology. At twenty-four he was ordained a priest. Five years later he was awarded the degree of Doctor of Theology.

Like John Huss, Martin Luther differed with policies of the Roman Church—except more so. Luther challenged the supremacy of the Pope. He spoke out against indulgence taxes. He said that everybody should read the Bible. And he said all should be allowed to sing in church.

Luther spent thirteen years translating the Holy Book into his native German language. He wrote thirty-seven hymns. And he outlined his contentions in ninety-five points and on October 31, 1517, nailed his theses to the door of the Wittenburg Castle Church for all to see. The Pope issued an edict for Luther's excommunication. Luther's writings were burned. Luther promptly burned the Pope's edict.

Martin Luther might have been the principal attraction at a public stake burning had he not had the foresight to gather about him powerful political leaders. But something had to be done with the heretic. Brought to trial at Worms, Luther was commanded by Emperor Charles V to retract. Refusing, he is said to have replied, "I cannot and will not recant. Here I take my stand. So help me God. Amen."

The court sentenced Luther. One elector, Frederick, the reformer's friend, was charged with keeping the prisoner in custody. Frederick turned his back while Luther translated the New Testament. Frederick looked the other way while Luther escaped to carry on his work of the Reformation.

Martin Luther and his followers were ever being hauled into court. He finally issued a formal protest against oppression—hence "Protest–ant." To give his followers courage on the eve of a bitter court battle in 1529, Martin Luther wrote this hymn:

A mighty fortress is our God,
A bulwark never failing;
Our helper He, amid the flood
Of mortal ills prevailing:
For still our ancient foe
Doth seek to work us woe;
His craft and power are great,
And, armed with cruel hate,
On earth is not his equal.

3. The Most Widely Sung Christian Stanza

Colleges in England were filled with rowdy characters. Winchester College was no exception. And the Roman Church and the Church of England were at such odds that when the Lord's Prayer was said at Oxford, the vice-chancellor sat down and put on his hat. But little student Thomas Ken thought things should not be so.

Sent through Winchester by his step-brother-in-law, orphan Ken went to Oxford for his degree, entered the Anglican ministry, and returned to Winchester as chaplain.

To encourage worship among his charges, Ken wrote a book which he titled *Manual of Prayers*. In his book Chaplain Ken admonished the boys: "Be sure and sing early in the morning and in the night season."

That was 1667. By 1674 the rowdy students were not singing early in the morning or in the night season, so Ken wrote three hymns and inserted copies of each into his manuals. His "Morning Hymn" began:

Awake, my soul, and with the sun
Thy daily stage of duty run;

> Shake off dull sloth, and early rise
> To pay thy morning sacrifice.

Thirteen stanzas followed. The last one reads:

> Praise God from whom all blessings flow,
> Praise Him all creatures here below;
> Praise Him above, ye angelic host,
> Praise Father, Son and Holy Ghost.

Chaplain Ken's "Evening Hymn" opened:

> Glory to Thee, my God, this night
> For all the blessings of the light . . .

It closed with the same stanza as did the "Morning Hymn": "Praise God from whom all blessings flow."

For those students who might awake in the night, Chaplain Ken wrote also a "Midnight Hymn." Like the other two, it also concluded with the stanza beginning "Praise God from whom all blessings flow."

There are many doxologies, but this simple four-line stanza is said to be sung more often than any four lines written since the psalmist David. The music is from a secular tune first used in Christian worship in 1551 to words of Psalm 134. In 1560 the tune was adapted to Psalm 100 and has been identified ever since as "Old Hundred."

The hymn "Awake My Soul, and with the Sun," found in many hymnals, is a selection from Thomas Ken's "Morning Hymn." But it is the closing stanza of his three hymns (with the word "angelic" changed to "heavenly") that has carried Thomas Ken's name through the ages.

In 1679 Mr. Ken was made chaplain to rollicking King Charles II.

In his efforts to persuade the merry monarch to mend his ways, Ken minced no words. But even with Ken's scathing remonstrances, Charles liked the little chaplain for "telling me my faults" and made him a bishop.

But Charles' successor, James II, sent Bishop Ken and six other churchmen to the Tower. The seven Bishops acquitted, King James left the country, and Queen Anne offered "little Ken" his old job. Tired of being made a bishop by one ruler, only to be thrown into prison by another, Ken moved to seclusion in the country.

Thomas Ken spent his last days in poverty. When he died at age seventy-four, in 1711, his possessions totaled an old lute and an old horse. Conforming with his request, the six poorest men in the parish carried his body to the grave.

As the sun rose, his friends lowered the casket and sang:

> Praise God from whom all blessings flow,
> Praise Him all creatures here below;
> Praise Him above, ye angelic host,
> Praise Father, Son and Holy Ghost.

4. A Favorite Hymn of the Pioneers

When your great-grandfather hitched his team to the surrey and ground over the dirt road to the meetinghouse, one of his favorite hymns was:

> Must Jesus bear the cross alone,
> And all the world go free?
> No, there's a cross for ev'ry one,
> And there's a cross for me.

When your great-grandfather's great-grandfather swung his musket over his shoulder and blazed a path through the thicket to the brush arbor two generations before the Colonies became a nation, he too sang those lines, for there were few other hymns in existence.

Rev. Thomas Shepherd, minister of the Church of England, wrote this age-old favorite in 1693. He wrote it, as was the custom of his time, for the concluding exhortation for one of his sermons.

The following year Shepherd changed over to the Nonconformists and preached in a barn for seven years until he could raise money enough to build a chapel for his congregation.

Mr. Shepherd's original lines began, "Shall Simon bear the cross alone, and other Saints be free?" But, as John Wesley would have later put it, "hymn tinkerers" have made minor changes to give us the present-day wordage. But the "tinkerers" have made only modest alterations, and basically the verses remain as Shepherd wrote them two and a half centuries ago—a decade before Charles Wesley, the most famous of hymn writers, was born.

The music to which Mr. Shepherd's verses are sung today is comparatively modern. American composer George N. Allen wrote the tune about the time Abraham Lincoln was riding circuits of Illinois as a young lawyer.

Almost a century older than the United States, "Must Jesus Bear the Cross Alone" is to church singing what sterling is to silver. It never grows old. It made its debut in a barn in England. Your great-great-grandfather sang it as he trudged through the wilderness. It is sung today in mahogany-walled chapels in Christian nations around the world. Perhaps your great-grandchildren will sing "Must Jesus Bear the Cross Alone" when they cruise in outer space from one planet to another.

> Must Jesus bear the cross alone,
> And all the world go free?
> No, there's a cross for ev'ry one,
> And there's a cross for me.

7

5. A Rebellious Youth Revolutionizes Congregational Singing

Line by line the clerk read a Psalm. Line by line the congregation sang after him. That is, everybody sang except young Isaac Watts.

After church services that Sunday in 1692, when his Puritan father called him to the carpet for not singing, Isaac said bluntly that there was no music in the Psalms. He said further that the Psalms didn't rhyme and that there was no sense in having to sing them line by line.

When outraged Deacon Watts's blood pressure subsided, he suggested that if his young upstart son were smarter than King David he might try his hand at writing something better. The result of that challenge was a revolution in church singing that has resounded for two and a half centuries.

Staid old Deacon Enoch Watts must have spoken without thinking when he hurled his sarcastic remark at his ugly little teen-age son. For at his boarding school in Southampton, the deacon himself had taught Isaac five languages before the boy was fourteen years old. That is, the deacon taught when he wasn't in jail for his acts against the Established Church.

And for twelve years Mrs. Enoch Watts had tutored her oldest son in the writing of verse. At seven he had won a copper medal for writing rhymes. He waxed so poetical that when the elder Watts threatened to flail him for rhyming even his everyday conversation, the boy cried out, "O father do some pity take, and I will no more verses make!"

Accepting his father's challenge, eighteen-year-old Isaac Watts set about "Christianizing" and "modernizing" the Psalms. His first attempt began:

Behold the glories of the Lamb
Amidst His Father's throne;

8

Prepare new honors for His name,
And songs before unknown.

The following Sunday the clerk read Isaac Watts' hymn. The congregation was so pleased that for two years Watts had to bring in one of his "modernized" Psalms every Sunday!

Eighteen-year-old Isaac Watts had successfully broken an ancient tradition. From his prolific pen would come "Joy to the World! the Lord Is Come," "When I Can Read My Title Clear," "Am I a Soldier of the Cross," and many another notable hymn.

With his bold departure from Psalm singing, Isaac Watts gave to Christianity a popular and inspiring medium of worship and paved the way for Charles Wesley, John Newton, William Cowper, and hundreds to follow.

Here is a hymn, written by Isaac Watts in 1719, that was one of three selections sung by President Franklin Roosevelt and Prime Minister Winston Churchill during devotional services aboard a British man-of-war off Newfoundland in 1941.

O God, our help in ages past,
Our hope for years to come,
Our shelter from the stormy blast,
And our eternal home!

6. "The Greatest Hymn in the English Language"

To attempt to single out any one hymn as the greatest ever written would create as much controversy as attempt-

ing to adjudge any one of the United States presidents as the greatest in American history.

Research in hymnology reveals marked differences in opinions even of the most qualified critics. But in the final analysis, public acceptance over a long period of time is as safe as any yardstick by which to measure the quality of hymns. For, after all, hymns were not written for critics. They were written for church congregations. And since many grand hymns have stood the test of time, the selection of any one narrows down to personal preference.

In England some years ago thirty-five hundred citizens were asked to list in order their one hundred favorite hymns. August Toplady's "Rock of Ages" led 3,213 of the lists. Yet poet Alfred Tennyson regarded Reginald Heber's "Holy, Holy, Holy" as the finest of them all.

Because few of the great poets have written hymns, some critics are reluctant even to regard most hymn writers as poets. Yet, after listing hymns by Bryant, Whittier, Holmes, and Longfellow, one critic selected Ray Palmer's "My Faith Looks Up to Thee" as being superior to them all. And Palmer was a minister. He made no special claim to being either poet or hymn writer.

Samuel Johnson charitably, and reluctantly, has mentioned Isaac Watts in his "Lives of the Poets." But the renowned critic apologized by saying that the little bachelor had only done "better what no man has done well." Another noted critic, Matthew Arnold, so admired the poetry of Watts that he sang and quoted "When I Survey the Wondrous Cross" on his deathbed.

And so go the opinions. Because they have stood the test of time, there are many "greatest" hymns. The one Matthew Arnold called "the greatest in the English language" is now two and a half centuries old. Inspired by St. Paul's declaration, "Far be it from me to glory, save in the cross of our Lord Jesus Christ, through which the world hath been crucified to me, and I unto the world" (ASV), Isaac Watts wrote the following lines in 1707.

When I survey the wondrous cross,
   On which the Prince of glory died,
My richest gain I count but loss,
   And pour contempt on all my pride.

Forbid it, Lord, that I should boast,
   Save in the death of Christ my God;
All the vain things that charm me most,
   I sacrifice them to His blood.

7. A Preacher's Visit Lasts Thirty-six Years

The Lord Mayor was there. Like other elite members of London's great Mark Lane Church, Sir Thomas Abney rarely missed a sermon by the renowned Dr. Isaac Watts.

Isaac Watts was young for the Mark Lane pulpit. When his health failed in 1712, he was thirty-eight, but he had been at the big church since he was twenty-six.

Watts was small—very small. He stood only five feet high. And his big head made his body appear even smaller. His long, hooked nose made his homely face even uglier. And he was sickly. Hardly had he seen a well day since smallpox nearly killed him when he was fifteen.

At Mark Lane, Dr. Watts rarely preached two Sundays in succession. But the congregation wouldn't let him quit. They employed an assistant and told Dr. Watts he could preach when he felt like it.

The disfigured dwarf was sought out by a beautiful lady who had come to love him through his poetry. Her name was Elizabeth Singer. Falling desperately in love, Watts proposed marriage to Miss Singer, but she shied away in disappointment. Abandoning hope of marriage, the little man wrote, "How vain are all things here below, how false and yet how fair."

Dr. Watts preached that Sunday in 1712, but he didn't feel like it. After the service Sir Thomas and Lady Abney invited him out to their mansion in the country. A week's rest, they said, would do him good.

At the Abney home, just out of London, Watts became attached to the three small daughters of his hosts. He wrote verse for them about the "busy little bee" and dogs that "delight to bark and bite." And he wrote a cradle song for them that began, "Hush, my dears, lie still and slumber; Holy angels guard thy bed."

In 1720 Watts collected his juvenile verse into the classic *Divine and Moral Songs for Children*. The book sold eighty thousand copies in a year, and six generations have been reared on it. His cradle song is still sung around the world.

Isaac Watts died, still a bachelor, at the Abney home in 1748— thirty-six years after going there for a week's rest.

A man with Watts's handicaps might have become bitter; but instead of dwelling on his own situation, he centered his attention on God. Out of his confidence in God's goodness and power, he wrote:

> Jesus shall reign where'er the sun
> Does his successive journeys run;
> His kingdom spread from shore to shore,
> Till moons shall wax and wane no more.

8. Neither Poet nor Composer Knew He Was Writing a Christmas Carol

Of the statues in Westminster Abbey, one is of Isaac Watts, the frail, sickly, gentle-mannered literary genius of the early eighteenth century. Another of the statues is of George Frederick Handel, the massive, robust, and hot-tempered genius of the keyboard and opera. Both men lived in London. Each knew the other. But neither suspected that their talents might someday be combined to produce one of the world's greatest Christmas carols.

It was in 1719 that Isaac Watts sat under a favorite tree on the Abney estate near London and wrote a hymn-poem based on Psalm 98. He was forty-five years old. In addition to a dozen books on various subjects, Dr. Watts, pastor of London's Mark Lane Church, had written and published six hundred notable hymns, among them being such immortals as "Come, We That Love the Lord," "When I Survey the Wondrous Cross," and "Alas! and Did My Saviour Bleed." But due to the dwarfed bachelor's infirmities, London's Lord Mayor, Sir Thomas Abney, took him into his home in 1712. There he remained for the rest of his life.

Twenty-two years after Isaac Watts wrote his hymn-poem on Psalm 98 and published it in his *Psalms of David Imitated,* a big, fat theatrical producer knelt in prayer in another part of London. He was George Frederick Handel, composer of some of the world's greatest operas.

As a boy in Germany, Handel had persuaded his father to allow him to pursue the study of music instead of law. Soon thereafter he was playing for churches in England.

13

A devoutly religious man, George Handel prayed and worked continuously for twenty-three days and nights in 1741 to compose his immortal oratorio *The Messiah*. It is such a superb masterpiece that for two centuries it has been drawn upon as the basis for scores of other compositions.

After extending his visit of a week to thirty-six years, Isaac Watts died on the Abney estate in 1748. He was buried at Bunhill Fields, but a statue of him was placed in the Poet's Corner of Westminster Abbey. There also stands a statue to the memory of a theatrical genius who never forgot God.

Almost a century later, in 1836, Boston's choir director-composer Lowell Mason drew upon Handel's *The Messiah* for music appropriate to the hymn-poem Isaac Watts had written in 1719.

And so, while the big statue and the little statue stand today in mute tribute to two geniuses of two centuries ago, tribute also is paid them every Christmas to the resounding echoes òf

> Joy to the world! the Lord is come;
> Let earth receive her King;
> Let every heart prepare Him room,
> And heaven and nature sing.

9. What Isaac Watts Was to England, William Williams Was to Wales

The Welsh are a singing people. They sing of great events; they sing of heroes in battle and of rolling hills and of the seas. Since as far back as the sixth century they have sung hymns—such hymns as there were in those ancient times.

William Williams was educated for a career in medicine. But he changed his course to that of the ministry. He might have become

a clergyman in the Established Church had he not been warned against such "fanatical dissenters" as John Wesley, George Whitefield, and Howell Harris, who preached in barns and cow pastures and on street corners.

Such warning was poor psychology for an inquisitive mind like that of William Williams. He straightway sought out the "fanatical dissenters." Williams found Harris preaching from a grave slab in a cemetery while worshipers turned their backs on their own preacher and filed out of their regular church service to hear his message.

Williams joined a branch of the dissenters called "Calvinistic Methodists." Unrestrained by formalities of the Established Church, the self-styled evangelist rode up and down Wales as John Wesley rode up and down England. He preached anywhere to anybody who would listen.

In forty-three years William Williams traveled 95,500 miles. His impassioned preaching drew crowds of ten thousand and more. Once he preached to a congregation of eighty thousand and noted in his journal, "God strengthened me to speak so loud that most could hear." He was bronzed by the sun. He was soaked by rain. He was chilled by snow, and he was beaten by mobs. But only death restrained his tongue at the age of seventy-four in 1791.

In England the people sang the hymns of Isaac Watts and later those of Charles Wesley, John Newton, and William Cowper. But the song-loving Welsh people had comparatively few hymns in their native language. So what Isaac Watts had been to England, William Williams became to Wales. He wrote eight hundred hymns for his countrymen to sing.

Given here is the hymn generally regarded as his best. Williams wrote it in 1745, but it became so popular that he translated it into English twenty-seven years later. Its popularity has held for two centuries.

Guide me, O Thou great Jehovah,
  Pilgrim through this barren land;
I am weak, but Thou art mighty;
  Hold me with Thy powerful hand;
    Bread of heaven,
  Feed me till I want no more.

10. A Mother Counsels Her Sons

"I wonder at your patience. You have told that same thing to that child twenty times," said the Reverend Samuel Wesley.

"Had I satisfied myself by saying the matter only nineteen times," Susanna Wesley replied, "I should have lost all my labor. You see, it was the twentieth time that crowned the whole."

The good Anglican minister of Epworth, England, marveled at his wife's seemingly inexhaustible patience with her nineteen children; he also marveled at her methodical upbringing of the nine she reared to maturity.

Each of the Wesley children had his well-defined chores. Each was awakened by the clock. Each learned to talk by repeating the Lord's Prayer. Each was taught the alphabet on his fifth birthday—not a day earlier, not a day later. And the first line each of the Wesley children learned to read was the first line in the Bible.

One day in 1735, after John and Charles Wesley were grown men, they journeyed from London to Epworth to seek their mother's advice. General James Oglethorpe had invited them to go to the new colony of Georgia as missionaries to settlers at Savannah.

While they were students at Oxford, the Wesley brothers had led an organization called the "Holy Club," which, it is said, was the beginning of the Methodist denomination. That is incorrect. The Methodist Church began at Susanna Wesley's knee when she rocked Charles in a cradle and held John on her lap while she patiently taught him to read, "In the beginning God created the heavens and the earth."

Returning from Georgia, Charles Wesley began a half century of hymn writing. John Wesley began his unprecedented preaching crusade. But neither would have made the voyage that changed the course of religious history but for the counsel of their mother. For Susanna Wesley told them, "Had I twenty sons, I should rejoice that they were all so well employed, though I should never see them again."

Charles Wesley has gone down in church annals as the "sweet bard of Methodism." Nobody knows exactly how many hymns he wrote. But none can deny that he wrote a greater number of stately hymn-poems than any other writer. It is generally estimated that his total output approximates sixty-five hundred. The one given here was written in 1747.

> Love divine, all loves excelling,
>   Joy of heaven, to earth come down;
> Fix in us Thy humble dwelling;
>   All Thy faithful mercies crown.
> Jesus, Thou art all compassion,
>   Pure, unbounded love Thou art;
> Visit us with Thy salvation;
>   Enter every trembling heart.

11. The Wesley Brothers Take an Ocean Voyage

The bow of the ship pointed to the mouth of the Savannah River, where Georgia and South Carolina meet on the At-

lantic. On board were two Englishmen. One was twenty-eight years old. He was private secretary to General James Oglethorpe. The other was thirty-two. He was on his way to Savannah, where he would serve as chaplain to the colonists.

Also on board the ship were twenty-six German immigrants of the Moravian faith. They were going to the Savannah colony, eighteen miles up the river, to worship God and to sing their hymns without fear of persecution.

That was early January, 1736. A storm overtook the windjammer while the Moravians were on deck singing hymns. The mainsail split. The mast broke in two. The seas pounded over the deck. Passengers ran, screaming, below. The Moravian Brethren didn't miss a note. Spellbound at the calmness of the Germans, John and Charles Wesley clung to the railing. After the storm John Wesley asked one of the Brethren, "Were you not afraid?" The Moravian replied, "Thank God, no."

Both John and Charles Wesley were clergymen in the Church of England. They never formally withdrew from the Established Church. But while students at Oxford, they disagreed with church policies and joined a club dedicated to the encouragement of personal religion. A methodical organizer, John Wesley wrote a set of rules and methods for the club. Fellow students dubbed the group "Methodists."

After a few months in Savannah, Charles Wesley returned to England. John learned enough German from the Moravians to translate some of their hymns and went up to Charleston where he published America's first hymnbook. Then he followed Charles back to London.

On the night of May 24, 1738, John Wesley visited a Moravian mission on London's Aldersgate Street. During the service, he wrote in his journal, "I felt my heart strangely warmed." Three days earlier Charles had experienced a similar "conversion." Religious history was in the making.

18

Charles Wesley preached in mining camps and prisons from Scotland to Wales. He wrote sixty-five hundred hymns. John Wesley swung into the saddle to carry his doctrine of "free grace" up and down England. He preached no less than forty thousand sermons in schoolhouses, barns, prisons, city streets, and cow pastures. And the Church of England closed its doors to what a contemporary called "those dirty, lousy Methodists."

On May 21, 1749, the eleventh anniversary of his conversion, Charles Wesley recalled a remark made by Peter Bohler, a Moravian leader. "Had I a thousand tongues," Bohler had said, "I would praise God with them all." Remembering Bohler's statement, Wesley wrote this hymn.

> O for a thousand tongues to sing
> My great Redeemer's praise,
> The glories of my God and King,
> The triumphs of His grace!

12. John Wesley Overlooks His Brother's Greatest Hymn

It was March, 1788. Eighty-year-old Charles Wesley had preached his last sermon at London's City Road Chapel. On the twenty-ninth friends gathered at his bedside. The crusader-preacher-poet sang Isaac Watts' hymn, "I'll Praise My Maker While I've Breath," and called for pen and paper. He would praise his Maker with yet another hymn-poem.

Returning to England from Georgia in 1736, where he had been secretary to Governor Oglethorpe, Charles Wesley with his brother

John began in earnest their religious crusade. In half a century John Wesley, four years older than Charles, traveled a quarter million miles and set England afire with forty thousand sermons. Mild-mannered Charles Wesley set the Christian world singing with sixty-five hundred hymns.

Charles Wesley wrote perpetually. Many was the time the "sweet bard of Methodism" stopped at houses along the road to ask for quill and paper that he might set down verses he had composed in his mind while riding from mission to mission. At thirty he wrote "Hark! the Herald Angels Sing," at thirty-nine, "Love Divine, All Loves Excelling," and at forty-one, "O for a Thousand Tongues to Sing." Hundreds lay in between. Thousands followed.

When pen and paper were brought to his bed, Charles Wesley was too weak to write. As his wife took down the lines, he began, "In age and feebleness extreme . . ." His last poem on paper, he whispered, "I'll praise . . ." and died.

Publishing a selection of his brother's works, John Wesley pleaded in the foreword that critics not "tinker" with the poems as "they are really not able to mend either the sense or the verse." But the plea has been ignored and "Jesus, Lover of My Soul" was tinkered with for a hundred years. Critics now concede that the original cannot be improved upon by tinkering, and the hymn is sung today just as Charles Wesley wrote it.

So great a masterpiece is this hymn that noted clergyman Henry Ward Beecher once said of it, "I would rather have written that hymn than have the fame of all the kings that ever sat upon the earth."

Many nice stories have been invented about the writing of "Jesus, Lover of My Soul"—birds flying through windows for refuge under Wesley's coat—storms at sea—and the author fleeing from mobs. The truth is that Charles Wesley was simply praising his Maker when, at thirty-one, he wrote this crowning masterpiece. But, strangely, John Wesley thought so little of it that he did not include it in his collection, and it did not appear in a Methodist hymnal until nine years after Charles Wesley died.

> Jesus, lover of my soul,
> Let me to Thy bosom fly,
> While the nearer waters roll,

While the tempest still is high:
Hide me, O my Saviour, hide,
Till the storm of life is past;
Safe into the haven guide;
O receive my soul at last.

13. A Great Easter Hymn Was Forgotten for Fifty Years

In addition to being one of the first English hymn writers, Charles Wesley was also the most prolific. His total output neared sixty-five hundred. John Wesley led one of the greatest evangelistic crusades in history. His sermons totaled approximately forty thousand.

It has been said that for fifty years neither of the Wesley brothers wasted a minute. John Wesley regularly retired at ten o'clock and was on the go at four every morning. He built a writing table and bookshelf in his buggy and wrote more than two hundred books and tracts while he traveled.

Charles Wesley wrote hymns morning, noon, and night. One day when his horse fell from under him, his arm was almost broken. But his prime concern was that his injured arm delayed his writing for a whole day. When he courted, at forty, he wrote love letters in the form of hymns. He wrote hymns on his wedding day.

In 1780 the Wesleys were past three score and ten. Charles was seventy-three; John, seventy-seven.

John Wesley held his brother's hymns in high esteem. He published them in his pamphlets and hymnbooks. But as the founders of Methodism grew into the sunset of life, John wanted to preserve the best of Charles' hymns in one great book. In the preface of his collection he pleaded that editors not "tinker" with nor alter any of his brother's poems, as they could neither "mend the sense or the verse."

But John Wesley might have served his cause better had he employed an editor. For he himself discarded "Jesus, Lover of My

Soul" and one Charles wrote in 1739, "Christ the Lord Is Risen To-day."

On his death bed in 1788, Charles Wesley whispered lines of a poem while his wife wrote it down. At age eighty-three John Wesley complained that writing fifteen hours daily was affecting his eyes. At eighty-six, two sermons every day tired him, so he reduced the number to seven a week. When he died, just short of ninety, in 1791, his passing was not caused by disease. Doctors said he "wore out."

In 1830, fifty years after John Wesley published his famous collection of his brother's hymns, an editor discovered "Christ the Lord Is Risen Today" and included it in the Wesleyan hymnbook. Charles did not write the Greek word "Alleluia" at the end of each line; a "tinkering" editor did that to make the verses better fit an old Easter tune. But perhaps John Wesley wouldn't mind, for otherwise the world would have been denied one of his brother's finest hymns.

> Christ the Lord is risen today,
> Sons of men and angels say,
> Raise your joys and triumphs high,
> Sing, ye heavens, and earth, reply,
> Sing, ye heavens, and, earth, reply.

14. A Printer Fills Out a Blank Space

The doors of every Anglican church in England were closed to John and Charles Wesley. The "dirty, lousy Methodists" might preach their Arminian doctrine of "free grace" in barns and pastures but not in a building of the Established Church. But apparently an eighteenth-century printer didn't know that.

22

For in need of material to fill out space in the Church of England's Book of Common Prayer, the craftsman took upon himself to insert a poem that began, "Hark, how all the welkin rings!" by an Anglican clergyman named Charles Wesley. It is said that attempts were later made to remove the hymn, but because of its popularity, it was allowed to remain. Thus this is the only hymn Charles Wesley ever wrote that got into the Book of Common Prayer of the denomination from which the author never officially withdrew.

Learning shorthand from scholarly John Byrom, Charles Wesley usually scribbled his hymn-poems rapidly. And he seldom took time to "polish" his works. "Hark! the Herald Angels Sing" has been edited so many times that few lines remain as Wesley wrote them. Nor in this case did he even bother to give his hymn a title; he merely wrote over the poem "Hymn for Christmas Day" and let it go at that.

Strange how some of the world's greatest hymns came so near fading into oblivion! For more than a century Charles Wesley's "Hymn for Christmas Day" was sung with mild enthusiasm to various tunes.

In 1840 Germany's boy wonder, Felix Mendelssohn, who wrote operas before he was sixteen, went to Leipzig for the celebration of the four-hundredth anniversary of printing. For the occasion Mendelssohn wrote an opera called *The Festgesang*.

In England, fifteen years later, a nineteen-year-old tenor named William Haymen Cummings was doing a bit of vocalizing on Mendelssohn's *The Festgesang* when the thought struck him that the second chorus of the opera could be adapted to Wesley's "Hymn for Christmas Day."

Written in 1738, this is one of Wesley's first hymn-poems. Scribbled hurridly in shorthand, without a formal title, it might have been lost but for a printer who used it to fill out blank space. Edited and re-edited and sung to various tunes for a century, the hymn stood a second chance of being forgotten. Then by chance being set to music written for a celebration having no connection with Christmas, "Hark! the Herald Angels Sing" has evolved into the most

widely sung Christmas hymn ever written. It is sung more than anything else Charles Wesley ever wrote.

> Hark! the herald angels sing,
>   "Glory to the newborn King;
> Peace on earth, and mercy mild;
>   God and sinners reconciled."
> Joyful, all ye nations, rise,
>   Join the triumph of the skies;
> With angelic hosts proclaim,
>   "Christ is born in Bethlehem!"
> Hark! the herald angels sing,
>   "Glory to the newborn King."

15. A Hymn Is Written to Replace a National Anthem

England's exhibition of naval and military might
in celebration of Queen Victoria's sixtieth year on the throne has
been called "the greatest show ever put on by mankind." Poets from
mainland and dominion paid homage in song to the seventy-eight-
year-old great-grandmother who by 1897 had broken all records for
continuous reign.

While many of the lyrical contributions were well written and appropriate, the London *Times* insisted that none but Rudyard Kipling should write the official Jubilee poem. But Kipling was in the
ill graces of the Queen because of one of his poems. Besides, the author's two grandfathers had been Methodist ministers, and the boast-
ful display of nationalistic pride was not in harmony with his sentiments.

Even as England reeled from her display of military might, Kip-

24

ling was quietly at work on a book he would call *Captains Courageous*.

The Jubilee came and went. Still the *Times* persisted. Unable to get into the spirit of the occasion, Kipling disregarded the request. But after repeated barrages of telegrams, the thirty-year-old poet-author put aside work on his book manuscript and wrote a poem for the London *Times*. The *Times* slapped it on the front page. It rocked the empire. But when the storm of protest subsided, a dazed nation settled down to ponder the sobering lines:

> Lord God of Hosts, be with us yet,
> Lest we forget, lest we forget.

Rudyard Kipling was not the first English poet to put militaristic pride in a secondary place. Two centuries ago the empire was singing a new anthem called "God Save Our Gracious King" to music of a German melody when another poet wrote an entirely different set of stanzas for the same music. But the poet's homage was to a greater King than England's George II.

In London, Italian orchestra leader Felice De Giardini thought the anonymous verses were so stately that they deserved music distinctly their own. So in 1769 De Giardini composed music just for the poem, and the world has been singing "Come, Thou Almighty King" ever since.

No one knows for sure who wrote the following hymn-poem. Most hymnals simply list the author as "anonymous." The author was perhaps not as indifferent to criticism as was Rudyard Kipling. And under the circumstances that inspired it, why the author did not sign it is understandable. There is evidence supporting the belief that it was the work of Charles Wesley. But whoever the poet, when he heard men singing praise to an earthly king, he wrote:

> Come, Thou Almighty King,
> Help us Thy name to sing,

Help us to praise:
   Father! all glorious,
O'er all victorious,
   Come, and reign over us,
Ancient of Days.

16. A Wandering Scribe Assumes the Role of Author

As late as a century ago printing was so cumbersome that when only a few copies of a literary work were desired, professional penmen were employed to prepare such copies by hand. And before the advent of the typewriter many authors employed copywriters to pen their manuscripts. Hence the profession of copywriting offered employment to many a scribe with a fair knowledge of spelling and a legible hand.

Some copywriters plied their trade in steady employment. Others roamed from city to city. Such a wandering scribe was England's John Francis Wade, who roamed throughout Western Europe, especially France and Portugal.

A craftsman of high order, proficient at copying music as well as Latin and other languages, John Francis Wade was in demand by choir leaders and institutions of learning.

But Scribe Wade tired of merely copying works of others. Two centuries ago he penned an "original" Christmas hymn that began:

Adeste, fideles,
   Laeti triumphantes;
Venite, venite in Bethlehem . . .

Wade also "composed" a fine piece of music for his Christmas hymn. But it has been said that the lyrics were sung in France be-

fore Wade was born. And the music sounds suspiciously like something the great George Frederick Handel might have composed.

But whether John Francis Wade plagiarized words or music or both, it is on record that "Adeste, Fideles" was included in a manuscript penned by Wade in 1750 for the English Roman Catholic College at Lisbon, Portugal.

In 1785 a copy of the Christmas hymn was sent to the Portuguese chapel in London. It was heard there by the Duke of Leeds, who promptly introduced the number to a group of concert singers he conducted. And from London Wade's Christmas hymn circled the globe.

Over a period of a hundred years "Adeste, Fideles" underwent no less than one hundred translations into English alone. In 1852 the hymn was given its present title, "O Come, All Ye Faithful," after a translation by Canon Frederick Oakeley, of Shrewsbury, England.

Whether John Francis Wade was the genuine author or whether the wandering scribe merely lifted the works of others, had Wade not inserted the Christmas hymn into a manuscript he copied for the Catholic College at Lisbon, the Christian world would have been denied this inspiring carol.

> O come, all ye faithful, joyful and triumphant,
> O come ye, O come ye to Bethlehem!
> Come and behold Him, born the King of angels!
>
> REFRAIN:
> O come, let us adore Him,
> O come, let us adore Him,
> O come, let us adore Him,
> Christ, the Lord!

17. An Infidel Turns to God

Joseph Hart spent the best years of his life denouncing the Bible and everything it stands for. Not content with merely being a nonbeliever himself, he devoted his marked literary talent to the spreading of propaganda against all religious faiths.

Attendance at church, with Joseph Hart, was for the sole purpose of finding fault and gathering themes for his venomous pamphlets. In reply to a sermon by John Wesley, Hart rebuked the founder of Methodism in a tract he called, "The Unreasonableness of Religion." In the town of Sheerness, where he taught languages, Joseph Hart became so obnoxious that citizens demanded that he leave town.

While infidel Joseph Hart was being invited to leave a town in England, Swiss-born Frenchman Jean Jacques Rousseau was being expelled from France for his outspoken views on politics. No less an infidel than Hart, Rousseau was an egotistic misfit who seemingly could get along with nobody.

Failing at several enterprises, Rousseau is said to have dozed off one day in 1752 and dreamed that he heard beautiful music. Awaking, he tried his hand at composing an opera. Its success so inflated Rousseau's ego that he was never able to compose anything else worth mention. At sixty-six he committed suicide.

Expelled from the town of Sheerness, Joseph Hart returned to his native London. One Sunday afternoon in 1757, when he was forty-five years old, the infidel teacher-writer wandered into a Moravian chapel to find more fault with religion. The preacher's text was from Revelation 3:10. God and the Moravian preacher did a remarkable job that Sunday. "I was hardly got home," Hart wrote of the sudden change that had come over him, when he "flung myself on my knees before God." He said he felt as if a "heavy weight" had been suddenly lifted from his shoulders.

Joseph Hart never wrote another pamphlet against religion. In two years he wrote enough hymns to fill a book, and he published the collection in 1759. Then he started preaching in an old frame building in London. When, eight years later, he died, twenty thousand people attended his funeral.

The strange birth of a hymn! Written by a converted infidel—sung to the music of a suicidal atheist!

Jean Rousseau's opera has been forgotten. The only music he wrote that survives today is that part of his opera which is sung to this hymn by Joseph Hart.

This, incidentally, was a favorite hymn of financier Cornelius Vanderbilt. Requesting its singing at his deathbed, the multimillionaire reputedly remarked, "I am poor and needy."

> Come, ye sinners, poor and needy,
>   Weak and wounded, sick and sore;
> Jesus ready stands to save you,
>   Full of pity, love and pow'r;
> He is able, He is able,
>   He is willing; doubt no more.

18. A Drunken Gypsy Sets a Youth to Thinking

The mischievous youth poured the old gypsy fortune teller another portion of grog and sat back to watch the fun.

When he was fourteen years old Robert Robinson's widowed mother sent him to London to learn the barber trade. His tutor-guardian was one Mr. Joseph Anderson. But the teen-ager cared lit-

tle for the tonsorial art, and when Anderson wasn't reprimanding him for acts of mischief, he was bawling him out for wasting time at reading books.

Now it was 1754. Robert Robinson had served his five-year stipulated apprenticeship, and barber Anderson was relieved of his devilish ward. Aware that he must earn his own livelihood, nineteen-year-old Robinson sought advice of a fortune teller.

Mischievously encouraged to drunkenness by the youth, the gypsy gazed groggily into her crystal ball and came up with a bit of advice that set her fun-loving client to thinking. Said she, "Young man, you will live to see your grandchildren." But she didn't say how long Robinson might live after becoming a grandfather.

Perhaps for the first time in his life, Robert Robinson realized that the time would eventually come when he must die. This realization and the thought that his grandchildren might regard his life as useless haunted him for months.

Robert Robinson was obsessed with these thoughts when in December, 1754, he stopped at an open-air revival to hear evangelist George Whitefield warn his congregation of "the wrath to come."

Finding peace by believing, the twenty-year-old youth soberly determined to devote his life to the ministry. And he prayed that when his time came to die he would go "softly, suddenly, and alone."

Armed only with his barbershop book learning, Robert Robinson began preaching as a Methodist. He later changed to the Independents and then switched to the Baptist faith.

Pastor of a small church at Cambridge, England, the self-styled minister became one of the empire's most forceful preachers. On June 9, 1790, when he was fifty-four years old, he went to Birmingham to fill the pulpit of the noted Dr. Priestly. The following morning Priestly knocked at his guest's door. There was no answer. Robert Robinson had died in his sleep—alone and, apparently, softly and suddenly.

Following the practice of ministers of his time, Robinson often wrote hymn-poems for conclusion of his sermons. He was only twenty-three years old when he wrote this hymn—just four years after the drunken fortune teller had set him to thinking.

> Come, Thou Fount of ev'ry blessing,
> Tune my heart to sing Thy grace;

30

Streams of mercy, never ceasing,
  Call for songs of loudest praise:
Teach me some melodious sonnet,
  Sung by flaming tongues above;
Praise the mount—I'm fixed upon it—
  Mount of Thy redeeming love.

19. A Slave Ship Captain Changes His Course

The old windjammer tied up at the dock in Southampton. She was a filthy ship. In her hold she had hauled many a cargo of human beings in bondage.

The captain staggered down the gangplank. Thoughtfully, he paused and looked back at his ship. Then he disappeared up the ancient cobblestone street. Youthful Captain John Newton had made his last voyage.

Captain John Newton was only twenty-three years old. But he had been to sea ever since his pious mother had died when he was only seven. After sailing with his sea-captain father, he had done a trick in the British navy. He had deserted, was caught, put in irons, and whipped in public. Defiant, the youth had signed on the lowest of all sea-going craft—a slave ship. Young John Newton hardly knew how to read. But he knew the sea, and it wasn't long before he was walking the bridge as master of his own slaver.

Captain John Newton wasn't drunk that day in 1748 when he staggered down the plank. He was sick. Stricken with fever, he was sick physically. And he was sick spiritually and morally. But most of all, he was sick of the slave traffic.

On a long voyage from Brazil, Newton had read a book called *Imitation of Christ* written three centuries earlier by Thomas a Kempis. Then came a storm that all but sent the captain and his ship to the bottom of the Atlantic. When the storm calmed, Newton began thinking about the Christ of whom the monk had written in his thought-provoking book.

Not an Englishman in the empire would have dreamed that Captain John Newton would have quit the sea for the pulpit. But when John Newton paused for a last look at his ship that day in 1748, that's exactly what his mind was set on doing.

After sixteen years at a land job by day and self-education by night, John Newton was ordained in the Anglican Church and sent to the little town of Olney.

John Newton became one of the most forceful ministers in England. But he never gave up his sea garb. In the sunset of life, as pastor of one of London's greatest churches, the one-time slave ship captain walked into the pulpit in the uniform of a sailor—with a Bible in one hand and a hymnbook in the other.

It was during his early years in the ministry, while serving the little church at Olney, that John Newton wrote this age-old favorite for the conclusion of one of his sermons.

Amazing grace! how sweet the sound,
That saved a wretch like me!
I once was lost, but now am found,
Was blind, but now I see.

20. A Troubled Poet Prays for His Soul

There was hardly a day during his sixty-nine years on earth that William Cowper did not suffer. Because of a weak constitution, he suffered physically. Because of uncontrollable spells of melancholia, he suffered mentally. Cowper could never dismiss from

his mind the belief that God had doomed his soul beyond redemption. This phobia drove him to attempts at suicide. Four times he was committed to insane asylums.

Cowper studied law, but he could not plead cases because of stage fright. And his speech was impaired by lisping and stammering. Yet when he had control of his faculties, there came from his pen masterpieces that have placed his name among the foremost of England's literary giants.

The world can thank, among others, the good Rev. John Newton —the one-time sailor and slave trader—for bringing out the best in William Cowper. While curate at the town of Olney, Newton gave the poet a home and put him to work. He built a study in the garden where the strange little man could write his poems, play with the rabbits, and talk to the birds. Newton encouraged and collaborated with Cowper in the writing of hymns for weekly. prayer meetings. Thus came into being the immortal collection, *Olney Hymns.*

Among these hymns are poems that are not only classics in English poetry but some of the finest Christian songs ever written, all because a big preacher with a big heart found a way to help a sick and wandering little poet. Though he made no claim to being a poet himself, John Newton wrote 284 hymns in the collection. William Cowper wrote sixty-seven, among them being "Oh, for a Closer Walk," "God Moves in a Mysterious Way," and "There Is a Fountain."

The latter hymn is omitted from some hymnals on the grounds that the metaphor "fountain filled with blood" is offensive. But apparently there are sufficient people whose appreciation goes beyond a tree to the beauty of the forest, and this grand old favorite has retained its popularity for a century and a half.

During the early part of the last century composer Lowell Mason cast about for poems to set to music for his Boston choirs. Among his selections was this poem by William Cowper, who had died in 1800 with a smile on his lips. Only half an hour before he died he expressed assurance that his prayers had been answered and that his soul had been at last redeemed.

> There is a fountain filled with blood
> Drawn from Immanuel's veins;
> And sinners, plunged beneath that flood,
> Lose all their guilty stains.

21. A Genius Works Between Spells of Insanity

At an orphans' school the larger boys bullied frail little William Cowper. As he grew older he developed a twisted outlook on life. As a man Cowper studied law but couldn't plead cases because of stage fright. A cousin found him a job as clerk in the House of Lords, but when Cowper learned that he would have to appear before a board of examiners, he suffered a nervous breakdown. But the thing that haunted William Cowper most, and eventually drove him to insanity, was his belief that God had closed the door of heaven to him.

William Cowper was released from St. Alban's Asylum in June, 1765. He wandered to the town of Olney, where he was taken in by Rev. John Newton, the converted slave ship captain.

Mr. Newton reasoned with Cowper. He set him to work visiting members of his parish and writing hymns for weekly prayer meetings. Thus was born the classic Olney hymns.

William Cowper was in and out of insane asylums four times. And between his spells of insanity, when he had control of his faculties, he wrote poetry that won for him the reputation of being the greatest poet of his time.

But Cowper could never completely shake off the belief that God had turned his back on him. At one time he hired a hack and went to the Ouse River, intent on drowning himself. But when the driver learned of his passenger's intentions, he drove Cowper back home.

Cowper tried to take his life with poison but failed. He once put a knife to his heart but faltered. He tried to hang himself with a garter. But the garter broke. God was not ready for William Cowper to die.

It was not until April 25, 1800, when he was sixty-nine years old, that William Cowper's time did come. And his passing was not by his own hand. Nor was William Cowper permitted to leave this life with the foolish notion that had plagued him for so many years. A clergyman who sat at his bedside has said that half an hour before the little poet died "his face suddenly lighted up with a look of wonder and inexpressible delight." God had not forgotten William Cowper. Just before he died the poet's face beamed with a smile, and he said, "I am not shut out of heaven after all."

It was on December 9, 1769, after reading in the book of Genesis, "And Enoch walked with God; and he was not; for God took him," that William Cowper wrote this hymn.

> Oh, for a closer walk with God,
> A calm and heav'nly frame,
> A light to shine upon the road
> That leads me to the Lamb!

22. An Old Sea Captain Speaks His Mind

The carriage drew up to a big church in London. A stooped and feeble man got out. He wore an old blue coat with big brass buttons. And he looked for the world like a broken-down old

sailor. The old man tapped his cane in front of his uncertain steps. He was led inside and up to the pulpit by a servant. Then the servant took a seat beside his master and studied some notes on a piece of paper while members of the elite congregation waited in hushed silence.

The good Rev. John Newton had been rector of Saint Mary Woolnoth for twenty-eight years. Before that he had held the pulpit of a small Anglican church in the town of Olney. At Olney, Newton had met poet William Cowper, who had been in and out of insane asylums and had tried more than once to take his life.

Mr. Newton took the little poet in and put him to writing hymns. He built a little house for the poet back of the rectory. Of the classic Olney hymns William Cowper wrote sixty-seven, among them being "There Is a Fountain" and "God Moves in a Mysterious Way." Newton wrote two hundred eighty-four of the Olney hymns, among them being "Amazing Grace," "How Tedious and Tasteless," and "Glorious Things of Thee Are Spoken."

Before Olney, Mr. Newton was a surveyor of tides during the day. At night he studied for the ministry. Before that he had read a book on the life of Christ and had been converted. Before his conversion John Newton had walked the bridge as master of one of the filthiest slave ships ever to ply the seas between the Dark Continent and slave marts of the world.

At eighty-two Mr. Newton's mind was almost gone. His memory came and went. But there were two things he never forgot. "I am a great sinner," the one-time slave ship master often said. "But Christ is a great Saviour," he said just as often.

The old man's sight was almost gone. A friend suggested that he retire because of his infirmities. The old man snapped, "What! shall the old African blasphemer stop while he can speak?"

Came time for the sermon that Sunday in 1807 at the great Saint Mary Woolnoth church in London. The servant quietly read the first item on the notes. The old preacher said, "Jesus Christ is precious." He paused.

The servant whispered the next item. "Jesus Christ is precious," Newton whispered in a broken voice.

"Yes, yes, go on," the servant whispered, "you said that once."

"I said it twice!" the old man snapped, "and I'll say it again! Jesus Christ is precious!"

Then the man who years before had boasted of his infidelity announced this hymn that he himself had written at Olney in 1779—the same year he had taken the great church in London.

> How sweet the name of Jesus sounds
> In a believer's ear!
> It soothes his sorrows, heals his wounds,
> And drives away his fear.

23. The Favorite Hymn of a Military Genius

The General was thirty-seven years old. He was six feet tall and well built. He wore a long beard, and his chestnut hair behind his high forehead was rarely combed. His boots were never polished. He wore an old slouch hat and a faded uniform with most of the buttons gone.

On the battlefield the General would have asked no quarter of the devil himself. But when he tried to lead prayer in church, he was so stricken with stage fright that his knees buckled and he had to sit down. But privately he was forever praying. He prayed so much that his men said of him, "When Old Jack ain't a-fightin' he's a-prayin'."

The General's religion bordered on fanaticism. He wouldn't even

drink water without first offering a prayer of thanks. He would neither read nor write a letter on Sunday. At the Virginia Military Institute in Lexington, where he taught natural science and military tactics, he held prayer meetings in his classrooms. He organized a Negro Baptist Sunday school and personally paid for its upkeep.

When the General wasn't fighting or praying, he was singing hymns. But he could hardly carry a tune; the simplest melody gave him trouble. But there was one hymn he could sing better than the others. It was his favorite. It had been written nearly a hundred years before by John Newton, the converted slave ship captain.

The General never took credit for his victories. Invariably he simply reported that "God blessed our arms with victory today." And his men made fun of him. They named four of his cannon "Matthew," "Mark," "Luke," and "John" because, they said, they "spoke the gospel." But, to the man, they would have charged the gates of hell if Old Jack had given the order.

The General marched his army of the Shenandoah fifty-two miles one day in 1862. When night came the army bivouacked in the Shenandoah Valley. And every man fell exhausted in his tracks with dread that he might be called for watch detail.

But when the cold grey of dawn broke, the men were awakened to a strange sound on the hill. There sat the General where he had watched over his men all night. With his old slouch hat in his hands, and his bearded face turned heavenward, Stonewall Jackson was singing as best he could his favorite hymn.

> Glorious things of thee are spoken,
>   Zion, city of our God;
> He, whose word cannot be broken,
>   Formed thee for His own abode:
> On the Rock of Ages founded,
>   What can shake thy sure repose?
> With salvation's walls surrounded,
>   Thou may'st smile at all thy foes.

24. An Immortal Hymn Is Born of an Argument

Perhaps the most popular legend about the writing of "Rock of Ages" has as its theme a wandering poet caught in a storm. Finding shelter under a cleft rock, the inspired poet is said to have penned his sentiments while the elements raged about him. But the trouble with this story lies in the fact that it was not invented until seventy-five years after the hymn was written. Actually, "Rock of Ages" was born of a much less dramatic occasion—an argument between two preachers.

"Arminianism" and "Calvinism" mean little to the layman today. But those were fighting words to many a theologian of two centuries ago. "Prize fighter" and "chimney sweep" were terms hurled by Arminian John Wesley at Calvinist August Toplady after the latter had accused the founder of Methodism of acting the part of a "lurking, sly assassin."

Thus the battle went. Both men, sincere in their respective beliefs, carried on their word battles in tracts, sermons, and hymns. Wesley contended that man could live without sinning and that grace was free to all. Toplady argued that all mortals were born damned and that redemption was a matter of God's selection.

While minister to French Calvinists in London, Toplady became editor of the *Gospel Magazine*. Thus he had an added outlet for his arguments. In March, 1776, editor Toplady wrote an article on spiritual improvement and the national debt. In the article he sought to prove that man was as helpless to pay his debt of sin as was England to liquidate her tremendous national indebtedness. At the rate of one sin per second, Toplady figured, a man would have chalked up 1,576,800,000 transgressions in half a century. But such a deficit of sin had been paid by Christ; so he admonished that men should

"pray afresh to God." A careful study of the poem that follows will reveal Toplady's theology.

As was the custom with ministers in writing their sermons, Toplady concluded his article with a poem. The phrase "Rock of Ages" came from the Bible. But it is interesting to note that his opponent, John Wesley, had published a hymn thirty years earlier with the opening line, "Rock of Israel, cleft for me."

Mr. Toplady died at the age of thirty-eight, two years after writing his article. John Wesley was still preaching his theology when he passed on at eighty-eight. But it is gratifying that this immortal hymn has outlived the age of heated arguments on theology during which it was born. Incidentally, Toplady's original title was not "Rock of Ages" but "A Living and Dying Prayer for the Holiest Believer in the World." But however immortal the words, this great hymn has been made greater by the music of Thomas Hastings, composer of more than a thousand hymn tunes.

> Rock of Ages, cleft for me,
>   Let me hide myself in Thee;
> Let the water and the blood,
>   From Thy wounded side which flowed,
> Be of sin the double cure,
>   Save from wrath and make me pure.

25. A Father Steps Down to Make Room for His Son

In 1758 a youthful minister took his place in the pulpit of the famed Baptist church on Little Wild Street in London. The young man had been assistant pastor there for ten years. Under the tutorship of one of the empire's most renowned clergymen, he himself was showing promise of becoming a great preacher. But at thirty-one, the young assistant felt a sense of meekness at filling the pulpit of his illustrious predecessor. Nevertheless, his instructor had insisted on the change, and the congregation accepted the recommendation.

No one knew better than young Samuel Stennett that he had a high standard to uphold. His father was a great minister. His grandfather had been one of England's foremost ministers and hymn writers.

Within five years after he took the pulpit at Little Wild Street, Rev. Samuel Stennett's reputation had spread across the empire. The University of Aberdeen conferred upon him the degree of Doctor of Divinity. Reformer Thomas Howard showered praise on his sermons. King George III was one of his most ardent admirers. Offers of even greater churches came. But the people at Little Wild Street would not let him leave.

Nor did Samuel Stennett want to leave. He had served his apprenticeship there. He had preached his first sermon there. So Dr. Samuel Stennett remained at Little Wild Street for thirty-seven years. When he died in 1795, he had never held another pulpit.

Had Joseph Stennett lived, he would have been proud of his son Samuel. For it was he who had given him the training at Little Wild Street. It had been he who had recommended his son to fill the great pulpit. And it had been he who had stepped down that his son might fill his place. The elder minister would have been proud to see his son surpass even his grandfather as a hymn writer.

Thirty-nine of Dr. Stennett's hymns were included in Dr. John Rippon's celebrated *Collection* of 1789. Two of the number are still found in almost every hymnal in the Christian world. Hardly a man living today does not know the one that begins, "On Jordan's stormy banks I stand, and cast a wishful eye to Canaan's fair and happy land, where my possessions lie."

But the following old favorite is generally regarded as Stennett's finest hymn-poem.

41

Majestic sweetness sits enthroned
Upon the Saviour's brow;
His head with radiant glories crowned,
His lips with grace o'er flow.

26. An Age-old Hymn Brings Comfort at the Gallows

The Union officer had been detailed to spring the trap, but he loathed the job. He fumbled at the rope. He waited for time. Like other Federal soldiers at Pulaski, Tennessee, he had grown to like the condemned Confederate youth. Turning to the thousand soldiers who stood with bared heads, the hangman offered all the money he had to anyone who would take his place. There were no takers.

Hoofbeats echoed in the distance. A courier sprang to the ground. The hangman rushed to meet him. Feverishly, he read the message from Union General Granville Dodge. It read, "Your side arms and an escort safely to Confederate lines for information of who gave you those papers."

At the court martial the General had explained to Sam Davis that the Federals did not want him nor any of the other captured scouts. The object of their having combed the hills of Tennessee had been the capture of the elusive leader of the spies, Confederate Captain E. Coleman.

"Had I a thousand lives," Sam Davis told the hangman, "I would lose them all here before I would betray a friend." Then he requested time to sing his favorite hymn, "On Jordan's stormy banks I stand, and cast a wishful eye . . ."

That was November 27, 1863. The hymn twenty-one-year-old Sam Davis sang on the gallows was then a century old. It had been written in London sometime prior to 1787 by Samuel Stennett.

After the execution other members of the Coleman Scouts were transferred by rail to a war prison in Illinois. But somewhere along the route, the tall, bearded former cell mate of Sam Davis escaped to carry on for his cause. In civilian life he had been a medical doctor, and his real name was H. B. Shaw. At the court martial Dr. Shaw had proved his identity and profession. But Sam Davis and the other scouts knew their leader as "Captain E. Coleman."

At Nashville there is a monument to Sam Davis. At Smyrna, Tennessee, the old Davis home is kept as a shrine to the memory of Sam Davis. And at Pulaski, Tennessee, on another monument to Sam Davis is this inscription, "Greater love hath no man than this, that he lay down his life for a friend."

Tall trees grow on the hill where Sam Davis was hanged on the outskirts of Pulaski. If you stand on the spot where the gallows stood and listen very closely as the wind blows gently through the trees, you can almost hear a young Confederate soldier singing,

> On Jordan's stormy banks I stand,
> And cast a wishful eye
> To Canaan's fair and happy land,
> Where my possessions lie.

> REFRAIN:
> I am bound for the promised land, . . .
> I am bound for the promised land;
> O who will come and go with me?
> I am bound for the promised land.

27. A General Dies While a Hymn Is Sung

It took a hard-boiled fighter to subdue hostile Creek Indians in the South, and Andrew Jackson was a hard-boiled fighter.

43

After conquering the Creek Nation, the hard-hitting general cut his way into New Orleans in 1815, rounded up recruits to add to his army of Tennesseans and, with six thousand men, slashed into British General Pakenham's twelve thousand veterans.

Burning with vengeance for ill treatment he had received as a youth while a prisoner of the British during the American Revolution, Jackson cut down two thousand English troops with the amazing loss of only seven of his own men killed and six wounded. But hard-boiled as "Old Hickory" was, he held in tender respect the religious devotion of his wife, whose favorite hymn was "How Firm a Foundation."

Nobody knows who wrote this hymn. It was first published in 1787, a year before Jackson settled in Nashville as a young lawyer and two years before George Washington became president. First published only under the initial "K," its authorship has been variously attributed to both George Keith and Thomas Kirkham. But it is doubtful that either wrote it. More likely the author was one Robert Keene, an assistant to London's Baptist minister and hymnal editor Dr. John Rippon, in whose book it first appeared under its original title, "Exceeding Great and Precious Promises."

At the Hermitage, just off the Lebanon Highway twelve miles from Nashville, lie the remains of President Andrew Jackson. It was there that the General once built a church and employed a preacher so that his beloved Rachael might worship God and sing the hymns she loved.

The brave warrior promised his wife that he would join the church. But Rachael died before the General got around to it, and after she passed on, Jackson lamented, "Heaven will not be heaven for me unless I find my wife there."

In 1845 a group of friends gathered at the Hermitage. "Old Hickory" was dying. He had forgiven his enemies—"collectively" (he so expressed himself when thinking of certain individuals), and he had joined the Presbyterian Church in Nashville. His former bitterness was gone, for he wanted only to join his wife in heaven.

44

"How Firm a Foundation" had been Rachael Jackson's favorite hymn. It had also become the General's favorite. Jackson asked the group at his bedside to sing it for him. And as they sang, the General died.

> How firm a foundation, ye saints of the Lord,
> Is laid for your faith in His excellent Word!
> What more can He say than to you He hath said,
> To you who to Jesus for refuge have fled?

28. A Humble Clergyman Is Richer than His King

A drayman stopped his cart at a two-room dwelling near a little Baptist church in the town of Wainsgate, England. It was there that young Rev. John Fawcett lived. The drayman pushed his way through the group of townsmen and started loading the few household goods of the youthful Baptist minister. For seven years Fawcett had served the little church, but now, at thirty-two, he was moving to London.

John Fawcett had been left an orphan when he was twelve years old. He had worked fourteen hours a day in a sweat shop. He had learned to read by candlelight, and he had studied hard. At twenty-five he was ordained and called to the small church at Wainsgate. The congregation numbered one hundred. His salary was one hundred dollars a year, paid partly in potatoes and wool.

It was a big promotion from the modest church at Wainsgate to the great Carter's Lane church in London. But Dr. Fawcett had

preached a trial sermon there, and the people wanted him. That's why the drayman had come with his cart.

John Fawcett was to become one of the empire's greatest scholars and clergymen. He was to publish an entire volume of hymns. He was to write books and establish a school for young preachers. His "Essay on Anger" was to so impress King George III that the monarch was to offer him "any benefit a king could confer."

The last article was loaded on the cart. The minister began his round of good-bys. There were the young he had married, the children he had held upon his knee, the old whose sorrows he had shared. They were simple people. Few could read or write. But their sincerity and devotion was too much for John Fawcett. He told the drayman to unload. He would stay at Wainsgate a little longer.

Dr. Fawcett never took the big church. He never left Wainsgate. He died there in 1817, fifty-four years later.

Renowned for his writings, awarded the degree of Doctor of Divinity, and admired by his king, Dr. Fawcett declined all offers to leave the simple people of Wainsgate. As for the king's offer, Fawcett called on the monarch only once, and that time to plead for the life of a parishioner's son under sentence to be hanged. King George granted the request. As for himself, the humble minister said that he "needed nothing a king could supply" so long as he was permitted to live among the people he loved—the simple people of Wainsgate whose devotion had inspired him to write this hymn.

> Blest be the tie that binds
> Our hearts in Christian love;
> The fellowship of kindred minds
> Is like to that above.

29. A Baby Girl Is Born to a Carpenter

Oliver Holden was a carpenter. And he was forever singing while he worked. He would put down his saw, beat out a few bars of a melody, and take up the saw again. In music Holden was never trained, but he was forever making compositions of his own. He had, in fact, won considerable fame for composing a welcoming song for George Washington when the General visited Boston in 1789.

At the age of twenty-one, carpenter Holden went from his native Shirley, Massachusetts, to Charlestown to help rebuild the town after the British had laid it in ruins during the Revolution.

But one day Holden failed to show up for work. Friends called at his home to learn the reason. They found Oliver Holden at his organ. He had become the father of a baby girl, and he had a song in his heart, a song he was making at his organ and putting on paper.

By 1793 Charlestown was rebuilt. Oliver Holden was twenty-eight years old. He put down his saw and turned to dealing in real estate. He was elected to the legislature. He opened a music store and built a Baptist church at his own expense.

Prospering in his various enterprises, Oliver Holden turned to publishing a complete hymnal under the title *American Harmony*. Searching for poems to set to music, he came across some verses in the English periodical *The Gospel Magazine*. But the poet had omitted his name—and for good reason.

England's Rev. Edward Perronet had preached and written hymns for the Wesley brothers during their religious crusade. But John Wesley and Perronet differed over laws of the Methodist church, and Wesley had banned Parronet's hymns from his songbooks. Mr. Perronet continued to write hymns under pen names and under no name at all.

Oliver Holden didn't know all that. He knew only that the unsigned verses he had found in the magazine exactly suited the tune he had written a few years earlier to celebrate the birth of his daugh-

47

ter. And the phrase "crown Him Lord of all" in the poem suggested the title "Coronation."

So Oliver Holden wedded the anonymous words to his music, and the Christian world got one of its finest hymns and a tune that has been used to many another poem. But perhaps John Wesley wouldn't mind because the Methodists are as fond of Mr. Perronet's hymn as are members of any other denomination, especially when it is sung to the tune carpenter Oliver Holden wrote to celebrate the birth of his daughter. ·

> All hail the power of Jesus' name!
> Let angels prostrate fall;
> Bring forth the royal diadem,
> And crown Him Lord of all.

30. The Oldest Surviving American Hymn

To avoid confusion, it should be noted that there were two men named Timothy Dwight: both were clergymen, both New Englanders, and both Yale presidents. The hymn-writing Timothy Dwight headed the institution from 1795 to 1817. The second changed the college to a university and was its president from 1885 to 1899.

As Stonewall Jackson held prayer meetings in his classrooms at Virginia Military Institute, so the first Timothy Dwight held revivals in the chapel of Yale. And for good cause. It was an age when Tom Paine's book *The Age of Reason* was sweeping the country, and a survey revealed that in the Yale student body only five men were professed Christians. President Dwight took to the chapel pulpit with a Bible in his hands.

Like Benjamin Franklin, Timothy Dwight was one of those sturdy Americans who could do a good job of almost anything he undertook. He was farmer, clergyman, editor, poet, legislator, orator, businessman, and educator. As one of his pupils put it, Dwight was "interested in everything" and his knowledge was "boundless." But Timothy Dwight's principal interests were the advancement of learning and the furthering of Christianity.

An avid Federalist, Timothy Dwight's principal hate was Thomas Jefferson's doctrine of democratic government. In a Fourth of July oration in 1800 the versatile Dwight wailed that mankind was being driven back to a savage state and that the country was being run by "blockheads."

While teaching oratory, literature, and theology, preaching to his students, and managing business affairs of Yale, Dwight also undertook the editing of a collection of Isaac Watts' hymns. Though his eyes had been dimmed by overwork and smallpox, he took the added task of writing thirty-three original hymns. Thirty-two of the collection have been forgotten, but one stands out today as the only hymn written in America during the two centuries after the Pilgrims landed on Plymouth Rock that is still in common use.

Besides making Christians of a spiritually confused student body, Timothy Dwight is remembered today for these three things: building a small college into a leading institution of learning, creating misery for Jeffersonian Democrats, and writing a hymn that promises to live longer than either Yale University or any political party.

> I love Thy kingdom, Lord,
>   The house of Thine abode,
> The church our blest Redeemer saved
>   With His own precious blood.

31. A Blind Composer Dictates a Tune

In one hand the wandering orphan carried a small bundle of clothes. In the other he clutched a roll of paper.

James Montgomery was born in Scotland in 1771. When he was six years old, his missionary father and mother placed him in a boarding school and sailed for the West Indies. Both died shortly afterwards.

At ten James Montgomery was writing verse; at twelve he failed in school; at fourteen he was working in a bakery shop; and at sixteen he was roaming the streets of English cities trying to sell his verse.

Wandering to Sheffield, the young poet was given a job on the weekly newspaper the *Sheffield Register*. But his hands were hardly soiled with printers' ink when the publisher became involved in political difficulties and fled to America. James Montgomery fell heir to the *Sheffield Register*.

Thus orphan James Montgomery had a publisher for his poems —himself. Changing the name of his newspaper to the *Iris*, he made the periodical a respected organ throughout England. Respected, that is, by all but government officials, who twice threw the young publisher into jail because of his outspoken political views.

On Christmas Eve, 1816, Montgomery published in the *Iris* a hymn-poem under the title "Nativity." Nine years later he changed the title to "Good Tidings of Great Joy for All People."

On April 30, 1854, now a worthy and respected citizen, the once roving orphan led his family in prayer at his palatial estate at Sheffield. That night he died peacefully in his sleep.

Thirteen years after James Montgomery died, one of England's greatest composers sat at his organ. Henry Smart had grown up in an atmosphere of music at his father's organ-building business. At twenty-two, young Smart did two things that were to influence the rest of his life. He became famous for composing the tune "Lancashire" (to which the hymns "Lead On, O King Eternal" and "From Greenland's Icy Mountains" are sung), but he impaired his eyesight by overwork.

At fifty Henry Smart had written 250 secular compositions and had edited two church hymnbooks—and he had completely ruined his eyes. Totally blind at fifty-two, Smart composed a tune he called "Regent Square" while his daughter put the notes on paper.

"Regent Square" has salvaged many a hymn-poem. For James Montgomery's "Good Tidings of Great Joy for All People" it has done more. Under its new title, "Angels, from the Realms of Glory," Smart's music has placed the one-time roving orphan's poem among the foremost of Christmas carols.

> Angels, from the realms of glory,
>   Wing your flight o'er all the earth;
> Ye who sang creation's story,
>   Now proclaim Messiah's birth:
> Come and worship, come and worship,
>   Worship Christ, the newborn King!

32. An Organ Breaks Down in Austria

Father Joseph Mohr was only twenty-six years old. But for three years he had been priest at the Roman Catholic church of St. Nicholas in the little Austrian town of Oberndorf.

Franz Gruber was thirty-one years old. Besides being schoolmaster, Gruber played the organ at Father Mohr's church when the antiquated instrument was in playing condition.

As concert artists, the Strasser sisters were known throughout Europe, their fame resting largely on their specialty of rendering mountain folk songs.

Except that he didn't always repair organs when he promised, little is known of an itinerant organ mechanic who made his headquarters in the city of Salzburg.

This ancient city lies in a valley in Austria between towering slopes of the Salzburg Alps. A few miles to the north lies the tiny village of Oberndorf.

During the week before Christmas in 1818, a group of wandering actors stopped at Oberndorf to give a play based on the Nativity. They would have given the play at the Catholic church, but the organ was broken down and the mechanic from Salzburg had parts strewn over the floor. So everybody in town, including Father Mohr, gathered in a home, where the play was given.

The sincerity of the actors moved Father Mohr. After the performance he strolled to a foothill of the Salzburg Alps that overlooks the tiny village.

It was a still night, a clear night, a holy night. So inspired was Father Mohr that in his mind he formed the lines of a poem that is destined to live as long as Christmas is observed by mankind.

Reaching home near midnight, the young priest put his poem on paper. It began, "Stille Nacht! Heilige Nacht!" The next morning he called at the home of Franz Gruber. He gave the musician his poem as a Christmas present and slyly suggested that the organist try his hand at setting it to music.

Came Christmas Eve night. Father Mohr met his flock at the little church. The organ mechanic was there, with apologies for not having completed his job. Franz Gruber was there, with his guitar and a tune he had written for Father Mohr's poem.

Gruber plunked the strings of his guitar. He motioned for the priest to come to his side. And there in the tiny Catholic church at Oberndorf, Austria, the two young men sang for the first time one of the most beautiful of all the Christmas carols.

So moved was the organ mechanic that he memorized both words and music. Back in Salzburg he sought out the Strasser sisters. The concert singers added the number to their list of mountain folk songs and sang it all over Europe. Thus "Silent Night, Holy Night" spread around the world. But it might never have gotten out of the Salzburg Alps had not an organ broken down in a little Catholic church in Austria.

> Silent night, holy night,
>   All is calm, all is bright
> Round yon Virgin Mother and child!
>   Holy Infant so tender and mild,
> Sleep in heavenly peace.

33. A Hymn Is Written While a Group of Men Talk

Sunday, May 30, 1819, was set aside by Protestant churches in England for emphasis on foreign missions. That's why a group of men had gathered the preceding Saturday evening at the vicarage at Wrexham.

In the group was Vicar Shipley's thirty-six-year-old son-in-law, Reginald Heber. Though born to wealth, Reginald Heber was one of the most generous, hard working, and brilliant clergymen in the empire. At Oxford his clean morals had been an inspiration to his classmates. He was so freehearted as a child that his mother had to sew his allowance in the lining of his clothes to prevent his giving away every cent on the way to school.

With his education, wealth, and cultural background, Reginald

Heber could have selected his pulpit. And that's what he did. He chose a small Anglican church in the town of Hodnet. For sixteen years he preached from the Bible, gave a fortune to the poor, and wrote fifty-seven hymns because, he said, he wanted to "draw more people to join in the singing."

Dr. Shipley planned a sermon on foreign missions, but he could find no suitable hymn on the subject. So he turned to Heber and requested that he write one. Retiring to a corner of the room, Reginald Heber wrote while the other men talked.

Dr. Shipley read the first three stanzas and said they were excellent. But Heber insisted on adding a fourth stanza to "make the sense complete." The next day Dr. Shipley's congregation sang about "India's coral strands" to the music of a secular song called " 'Twas When the Seas Were Roaring."

That might have been as far as Heber's hymn was destined to go except for an incident that happened in America. The following February, in Savannah, Georgia, a Miss Mary Howard read Reginald Heber's missionary poem in the *Christian Observer*. She wanted to use the verses at her church but could find no suitable tune. Then she thought of a twenty-eight-year-old bank clerk who directed choirs and wrote music as an avocation. As only Lowell Mason could do, he set Reginald Heber's poem to music in less than half an hour while Miss Howard waited.

Six years later Bishop Reginald Heber died in India, where there are no coral strands. Lowell Mason gave up his bank job in Savannah and went to Boston to spend forty-five years directing choirs, publishing hymnbooks, and composing.

Here is the poem Reginald Heber wrote in the corner of a living room at Wrexham, England, one Saturday night while a group of men talked on the subject of foreign missions.

> From Greenland's icy mountains,
> From India's coral strand,
> Where Africa's sunny fountains
> Roll down their golden sand,
> From many an ancient river,
> From many a palmy plain,
> They call us to deliver
> Their land from error's chain.

54

34. A Hymn Is Found in an Old Family Trunk

Reginald Heber loved the quiet town of Hodnet. With his inherited wealth, his Oxford education, and his family background, the young Anglican minister could have lived in a London mansion. Instead, he built a mansion at Hodnet, preached at the little church there, and gave of his wealth to the poor.

Heber was not strong. Perhaps that's the more reason why he loved the relaxed life of the small town. His congregation too was small, and he had time to write articles for periodicals and hymns for his church. "My Psalm-singing continues bad," he wrote a friend. Others were singing the songs of Wesley, Cowper, and Watts; but the Bishop of London said the time was "not yet ripe" for the singing of hymns in the Established Church. So Heber wrote his own hymns and used them on special occasions. He wanted to publish them in a book, but the bishop frowned on the idea, and Heber put his poems away in an old family trunk.

Came 1823. Reginald Heber himself became a bishop. His superiors wanted him to take charge of the Calcutta area, but he didn't want to leave Hodnet. Twice he declined. On the third request he gave in, saying that a preacher is like a soldier—he must obey his superiors. He went to India and for three years tried to serve the vast territory. Long travels and strenuous work taxed his strength. And the air was so hot, he commented, that it felt as though it "blew in from a furnace."

On April 3, 1826, at the age of forty-three, the young Bishop went to preach at Trichinopoly. The crowd was so large that he had to stand on the mission steps and deliver his sermon in the open in the hot sun. That afternoon he plunged into a pool of cool water. He suffered a stroke and drowned.

Heber's widow found the roll of hymns in the trunk and had them published. In 1861 a London publisher and his staff were studying the poems when they came across a masterpiece. Composer John Dykes was called in. Dykes, with three hundred fine compositions to his credit, could compose music almost anywhere. He wrote on city streets, on trains, and in railroad stations. So a mere conference of editors was no distraction for John Bacchus Dykes. And, like Lowell Mason, he wrote rapidly. When he left the publisher's office, he left a group of startled men and one of the finest hymn tunes ever composed.

Words and music, here is one of the most majestic hymns in any book. But how different were poet and composer! When John Dykes differed with the bishop of London, he promptly took his case to court.

Reginald Heber wrote fifty-seven hymns. He might have written more had he not died trying to please his bishop. This, Heber's greatest, was written especially for his congregation at Hodnet.

> Holy, holy, holy! Lord God Almighty!
>   Early in the morning our song shall rise to Thee;
> Holy, holy, holy, merciful and mighty!
>   God in three Persons, blessed Trinity!

35. An Organist Leaves Church in Disgust

I once overheard a member of my father's congregation make excuses for habitual absence from church. "But," the man hastened to explain, "I am always there in spirit."

"That's fine," replied my Methodist-minister father. "But most of

my flock come in person. That spares me the feeling of stupidity that comes with preaching to a congregation of spirits."

On a rainy Sunday in 1849 Dr. Hiscox's congregation at the Central Baptist Church in Norwich, Connecticut, was comprised mostly of "spirits." Hiscox had prepared a series of sermons on "The Words on the Cross," but on that dismal sabbath, most of the members attended only in spirit. Of the choir only the leading soprano, Mrs. B. S. Rathbun, was there in person. So humiliated was organist Ithamar Conkey that he put on his hat, left by a back door, and went home in disgust.

England's Sir John Bowring was one of the most brilliant men in the British empire. Son of a wealthy exporter of woolen goods, John Bowring could speak five languages when he left school at sixteen to represent his father in foreign markets. Before he died, at eighty, it is said that Sir John could speak two hundred languages!

Twice a member of Parliament, awarded the LL.D. degree, knighted by the queen, and made governor of Hong Kong, Sir John Bowring wrote thirty-six books on diversified subjects ranging from religion to politics. But save for a small collection of hymns, all his writings have been forgotten. The best of his hymn-poems, one based on the verse, "But God forbid that I should glory, save in the cross of our Lord Jesus Christ" (Gal. 6:14), might also have been forgotten had not an organist in Connecticut left church in disgust one rainy Sunday in 1849.

Remorseful for having deserted his preacher, organist Conkey pondered Dr. Hiscox's sermons on "The Words on the Cross." He recalled Sir John Bowring's hymn, "In the Cross of Christ I Glory." The music was not very good, and Conkey's choir never sang the number with enthusiasm. The words were magnificent, thought the organist, but for want of a better tune he feared the hymn might eventually die. So while the rain came down that Sunday afternoon, Ithamar Conkey wrote a new tune for Sir John Bowring's poem. He named the composition "Rathbun" in honor of the lone choir member who had showed up in person that morning rather than sending her "spirit" to sing in the choir.

> In the cross of Christ I glory,
>   Tow'ring o'er the wrecks of time,
> All the light of sacred story
>   Gathers round its head sublime.

57

36. A Carriage Wheel Maker Teaches His Children to Sing

As he traveled about his native Austria, the carriage wheel maker was forever singing. And as each of his twelve children grew old enough to read music, he taught them to sing. His son Franz Joseph could sing so well at the age of eight that the chapel master at Vienna put him in the choir at St. Stephens. But when Franz Joseph reached the age of sixteen, his voice changed, and his younger brother, Johann Michael, took his place in the choir. Thus began two notable careers, from which came some of the world's finest musical compositions.

Both Franz Joseph and his brother Michael devoted much of their time and talent to the church. Johann Michael Haydn is credited with no less than 360 religious compositions. And the great Franz Joseph Haydn once said, "I know God has bestowed a talent upon me, and I thank Him for it. I think I have done my duty . . . let others do the same."

Johann Michael Haydn was past middle age in 1779 when a boy named Robert Grant was born in Scotland to a member of Parliament. Some say Robert Grant was born in India in 1785 while his father was chairman of the East India Company.

Robert Grant followed his father to Parliament. He became a director in the East India Company. At fifty he was made governor of Bombay. The elder Grant had encouraged missions in India. Robert Grant did more. He supported missions, and he wrote hymns for the missionaries to sing.

Sir Robert Grant was not a prolific writer of hymns. But he wrote

well. In 1839, a year after he died in India, his brother Charles had twelve of his hymn-poems published in a little volume entitled *Sacred Poems.*

For want of suitable music, most of Robert Grant's hymns have been forgotten. But one stands out today as one of the most stately hymns ever written. But even it might have been forgotten had it not been adapted to a composition written by Johann Michael Haydn.

Based on the Psalm 104, here is a hymn written by Sir Robert Grant, governor of Bombay. It is sung to music written by the son of a humble carriage wheel maker who loved music and taught his children to sing.

> O worship the King, all glorious above,
> And gratefully sing His wonderful love;
> Our Shield and Defender, the Ancient of Days,
> Pavilioned in splendor, and girded with praise.

37. A Busy Youth Scribbles a Poem in Half an Hour

Like Lowell Mason, who was forever hurrying about Boston composing music, publishing hymnbooks, and directing choirs, Boston's Samuel Francis Smith was always busy.

It was in early 1832 that a civic-minded Bostonian, William C. Woodbridge, gave composer Lowell Mason a batch of songs he had brought back from Germany. Woodbridge had picked up the assortment while studying European school systems and thought Mason might translate some of them for use in his choir work.

59

Lowell Mason thought some of the music showed promise. But, to him, the words might as well have been written in Egyptian hieroglyphics. Then he remembered young Samuel Francis Smith, the ministerial student and Harvard graduate who was noted for his ability to speak fifteen languages.

Samuel Francis Smith lived in the shadow of the church where the lantern was hung on the night Paul Revere made his famous ride. So Smith naturally absorbed a liberal share of patriotism. It was, according to Smith's account, half an hour before sundown on February 2, 1832, that he got around to translating one of the German songs for Mason. The piece was under the patriotic title (in German) "God Bless Our Native Land." Smith probably didn't know that England had been using the same tune to "God Save the King" for a hundred years. But why translate the German words? He took a piece of paper "six inches long and half as wide," and by the time the sun was over the horizon, he had written some original patriotic verses about America. In a Boston park, the following July Fourth, Lowell Mason's childrens' choir sang "My Country 'Tis of Thee" for the first time.

On November 16, 1895, a noted Baptist minister hurried, as always, to catch a train. He was on his way to fill a preaching engagement. Besides writing books, teaching languages at Newton Center, and holding numerous posts of his denomination, Dr. Smith was also the author of a hundred and fifty hymns.

The train had started to move when the conductor quickly signaled the engineer to stop. Something had happened on the platform of one of the coaches. Perhaps the old gentleman had taken the steps too spryly for his eighty-seven years. But whatever the cause, Samuel Francis Smith was dead. He had died as he had lived—in a hurry—on the go.

Of all his works, Dr. Smith is remembered best for his missionary hymn "The Morning Light Is Breaking" and for the following poem he scribbled on a small scrap of paper when he was twenty-six years old.

> My country, 'tis of thee,
>   Sweet land of liberty,
> Of thee I sing:
>   Land where my fathers died,

Land of the pilgrims' pride,
From every mountain side,
Let freedom ring!

38. A Secular Tune Saves a Fine Missionary Hymn

Like England's William Carey, American pioneer missionary Adoniram Judson lit his own lamp and found his own path.

A century and a half ago Protestant foreign missions was in its infancy. Among others early in the field, dauntless Adoniram Judson worked in Burma for fifteen years with little encouraging results. Many a man of lesser courage would have given up in despair, but in 1829 the courageous missionary reported to the Baptist Missionary Union in America that "the light is breaking."

While Adoniram Judson was working in Burma, Boston's Samuel Francis Smith was studying for the ministry at Andover Theological Seminary. Smith reputedly knew fifteen languages. He could write poetry. And he was engrossed in the foreign missions movement.

While translating a number of foreign songs for choir director Lowell Mason, Smith had come across a German tune he liked and wrote some verses for it that started Americans to singing "My Country, 'Tis of Thee." That was in February, 1832. That same month, after reading Adoniram Judson's report, Smith wrote a poem about the light breaking on foreign mission fields. Though he lived to a ripe old age and wrote prolifically for more than sixty years, it is singular that two poems he wrote in the same month as a young man have outlived all his other works.

While Judson was in Burma, and while Smith was writing poems, a young Englishman named George James Webb, son of a wealthy farmer, was crossing the Atlantic to try his luck at writing secular songs in America. To pass time on the boat, Webb wrote a song he called " 'Tis Dawn, the Lark Is Singing." He had no more thought

of composing a hymn tune than he had of swimming the rest of the way to America.

Samuel Smith's missionary hymn was sung to first one tune and another for nearly thirty years, but it never seemed to take hold. Then in 1861 composer William Bradbury, a student of Lowell Mason, adapted Samuel Smith's hymn-poem to the secular tune George Webb had written on board ship. The music became so popular that soldiers of the Union Army began singing the words of "Stand Up, Stand Up for Jesus" to the same tune. And both hymns have been sung to George Webb's secular music ever since.

Soon after boarding a train in Boston in 1895 Dr. Samuel Smith collapsed and died before the train left the station. Of his one hundred fifty hymn-poems his best was inspired by missionary Adoniram Judson's report about the light breaking in Burma. But it might have been forgotten long ago had it not been wedded to music written for a song about a lark singing at dawn.

> The morning light is breaking;
> The darkness disappears;
> The sons of earth are waking
> To penitential tears;
> Each breeze that sweeps the ocean
> Brings tidings from afar
> Of nations in commotion,
> Prepar'd for Zion's war.

39. A Bank Clerk and a Shoe Clerk Stop for a Chat

It is, perhaps, natural to place first importance upon the author of the words of a hymn. The fact is, however, that many a stately hymn-poem might have been entirely forgotten but for the work of those noble craftsmen who composed the music. And no man in the history of hymn writing has contributed more in this respect than the dean of American hymn tune composers— Lowell Mason.

One day in 1832 two men stopped in front of a store in Boston. One was Lowell Mason, near middle-age and recently from Savannah, Georgia, where for sixteen years he had directed choirs and clerked in a bank. The other man was twenty-four-year-old Ray Palmer, recent graduate of Yale and clerk in a dry goods store.

Three years later Mason was to be awarded the first Doctor of Music degree to be conferred by an American college. That same year, 1835, Ray Palmer was to be ordained a minister in the Congregational Church and was later to publish several volumes of verse.

Lowell Mason was one of the busiest men in Boston. He was directing three choirs, hounding the city board of education to put a course of music in the schools, and compiling material for his *Spiritual Songs for Social Worship*. That's why he stopped Palmer on the street. He wanted him to write some verses for his new song book.

For ten years Ray Palmer had burned the candle at both ends; at times he wondered if he could go on. While teaching at a girls' school and studying for the ministry, he almost gave up. One night at his boarding house he wrote a poem in a little moroccobound notebook, just to read for renewed courage.

When Mason asked Palmer to write something for his hymnal, the ministerial student showed him the poem he had carried in his pocket for two years. The composer hurried into a nearby store, borrowed a piece of paper, and copied the poem. Handing the little book back to Palmer, Mason said, "Mr. Palmer, you may do many good things, but posterity will remember you as the author of 'My Faith Looks Up to Thee.' "

That night in his studio Lowell Mason set to music Dr. Palmer's first and greatest hymn. And Lowell Mason was right. Dr. Ray Palmer has gone down in history because of that one poem he wrote in his notebook just to read to bolster his faltering courage. But however stately might be the words, credit is due also to Lowell Mason for composing a tune so appropriate as to insure the immortality of these words.

> My faith looks up to Thee,
>   Thou Lamb of Calvary,
> Saviour divine!
>   Now hear me while I pray,
> Take all my guilt away,
>   O let me from this day
> Be wholly Thine!

40. A Soldier Looks Under a Carpet

The Humphreys household in Dublin, Ireland, was accustomed to strict discipline. The father was an officer in the Royal Marines, and members of the family accepted his methodical regulations as a matter of course. Perhaps that's why nine-year-old Cecil Frances Humphreys slipped away to the privacy of a back room to write her poems. Then, too, being near-sighted, the little girl had become timid and shy.

One day in 1832 Squire Humphreys noticed a bulge in the floor

covering. Lifting the carpet, he discovered a small batch of papers on which his daughter had written verse. As he read the childish literary efforts, he became increasingly interested. Humphreys was a soldier, but there was something touching in the lines. He slipped the papers into his pocket and called at the study of his friend John Keble. The renowned clergyman-poet told Humphreys that his child was a born writer.

The following Saturday evening soldier Humphreys called the household together. He proudly read aloud Cecil's poems. And he announced that the family would gather every Saturday evening thereafter, at which time he would read any poems Cecil might have written during the week.

Thus encouraged by her father, when Cecil Frances Humphreys was twenty-five, she published her delightful *Hymns for Little Children,* which, it is said, has never been surpassed by a similar collection and for which the great John Keble himself wrote the introduction.

In 1850 the poetess married an Irish clergyman, William Alexander, who once said of his wife, "From one poor home to another, from one sick bed to another, from one sorrow to another, she went." Yet the busy little near-sighted woman found time to raise a family, teach Sunday school classes, and to write four hundred hymns, among which is the well known "Jesus Calls Us o'er the Tumult," which she wrote in 1852.

It was in 1848 that Mrs. Alexander wrote her best hymn. She tried to explain the Apostle's Creed to a sick little girl, but the child could not understand the phraseology. So Mrs. Alexander simply put the creed into a poem for children.

When Cecil Frances Alexander was buried in Londonderry in 1895, "The Green Hill" was sung at her funeral. Though he had risen high in the Anglican Church, Archbishop Alexander said he would be remembered only as the husband of his noble wife. And when the noted churchman died in 1911, there was sung also at his funeral the hymn his wife had written sixty-three years earlier at the bedside of a little girl.

There is a green hill far away,
    Without a city wall,
Where the dear Lord was crucified,
    Who died to save us all.

REFRAIN:
Oh, dearly, dearly has He loved,
    And we must love Him, too,
And trust in His redeeming blood,
    And try His works to do.

41. A Composer Dodges London Traffic

Rev. John Bacchus Dykes could compose a melody in a thunderstorm. Of the three hundred hymn tunes to his credit, many were written in crowded railway stations, on trains, and even in the pulpit while he waited to deliver his sermons. So neither rumbling carriages nor clattering hordes of humanity interrupted his thoughts as he hurried along the streets of London one day in the summer of 1865.

Composer-minister Dykes was running through his mind a poem he had read in an old March, 1834, issue of the *British Magazine*. The poem had been under the title "Faith, Heavenly Leadings"

and had been written in June, 1833, by a disturbed young church-man named John Henry Newman.

At Oxford, John H. Newman had been a leader in the Oxford Movement. At twenty-seven he became a vicar in the Church of England. But like many another clergyman of the day, he was dis-appointed at the apathy of church leaders. He denounced the Roman Catholic Church and then pondered joining it. He was, in brief, confused. He was so confused that by the time he was thirty the indecision had shattered his health, and he took a trip to Italy for rest.

In Italy he was stricken with fever and was confined to bed for three weeks. He waited three more weeks for a ship returning to his native England. When, finally, he found passage on a fruit ship, the vessel stopped in the Mediterranean. The sails hung limp on the masts. For a week not a breeze stirred. The prospect of starving at sea, save for the oranges on the ship, added to his homesickness, depression, and physical exhaustion, so John Henry Newman went below to his cabin and wrote his immortal prayer-poem. Two weeks later the ship docked. Twelve years later Newman made up his mind. He went over to the Catholic faith in which, at seventy-eight, he became a cardinal.

Cardinal Newman had no thought of his poem's being used as a hymn. He once wrote that "the words are not suitable for singing." Yet this is regarded by many critics and poets, notably Alfred Tennyson, as being the finest hymn ever written. Robert Guy McCutchan, an authority on hymns, has said, "No more beautiful hymn, nor one more dignified, has been written in English."

When composer John Bacchus Dykes reached his study that August day in 1865, Newman's immortal lines were wedded to an immortal tune written on the noisy streets of London. And Cardinal Newman always insisted that it was Dykes' music that made the hymn so popular. "You see it is not the hymn," he told a friend, "but the tune that has gained the popularity."

However fine might be the tune, one has but to read thought-fully Newman's lines to realize that the Cardinal was entirely too modest in his statement.

> Lead, kindly Light! amid th' encircling gloom,
> Lead Thou me on;

The night is dark, and I am far from home,
   Lead Thou me on;
Keep Thou my feet;
   I do not ask to see
The distant scene;
   One step enough for me.

42. A Cabinetmaker Takes Up Writing

"On Christ, the solid Rock, I stand; All other ground is sinking sand." Those words ran over and over like a refrain in the mind of a thirty-four-year-old London cabinetmaker as he walked up Holborn Hill toward his wood-working shop.

Cabinetmaker Edward Mote was a happy man. He had learned his trade, and he loved his work. For years he had worked for wages, but now he owned his own shop. And Edward Mote also had a hobby. He spent his spare hours writing articles, and now and then a London periodical published them. When a key line came to his mind, Mote even tried his hand at writing poems.

Most of all, Edward Mote was happy because his once-confused mind had become fixed on his belief in God. He had been brought up in a house where the Bible was not permitted. His playground had been the streets of London. But after he became a man he attended Tottenham Court Road Chapel, where sermons of the renowned John Hyatt had set his mind at ease.

Edward Mote's cabinet shop ran itself that day in 1834. He had a key line for a poem, and he wanted to set it down on paper while

the inspiration was fresh. So while his workmen went about their jobs, Mote closeted himself in his office. He wrote the caption "Gracious Experience of a Christian." Then he went to work on the verses. As he put it, "In the day I had four verses complete and wrote them off."

On the following Sunday Edward Mote visited the home of a minister friend whose wife was near death. Groping for consoling words, he thought of his poem. He quoted the lines to the dying woman, and at the conclusion of each verse he added his key line, "On Christ, the solid Rock, I stand; All other ground is sinking sand." He later had a thousand copies of his poem printed for distribution among friends. A hymnal editor came into possession of one of the leaflets, and "The Solid Rock" has been sung ever since.

Edward Mote gave up his cabinet shop. He entered the Baptist ministry at the age of fifty-five. He built a Baptist church at his own expense. When the congregation offered to deed the property to him, he said, "I only want the pulpit, and when I cease to preach Christ, turn me out of that."

At seventy-seven, in 1874, Edward Mote looked up at friends at his bedside and said, "The truths I have preached will do to die upon." So passed a man who had been reared in a godless home, had learned a trade, and had given it up for the ministry. But his memory has lived for generations because he took time off one day from running his wood-working shop to write these lines further made immortal by music composed for them by William Bradbury, a student of Lowell Mason.

> My hope is built on nothing less
> Than Jesus' blood and righteousness;
> I dare not trust the sweetest frame,
> But wholly lean on Jesus' name.
>
> REFRAIN:
> On Christ, the solid Rock, I stand;
> All other ground is sinking sand,
> All other ground is sinking sand.

43. An Invalid's Mite Becomes a Windfall

The doctor stopped his carriage at the home of the Anglican minister at Brighton, England. But there was nothing in his medicine kit that could help the paralyzed sister of Rev. Henry V. Elliott. He was calling merely to offer a word of cheer and to leave one of the little leaflets he had bought to distribute among his shut-in patients.

The leaflets were selling all over England, the doctor said. They were even being translated into foreign languages—and for good cause. Someone had written a poem to help finance the building of a school for children of poor clergymen. It said so at the top of the page: "Sold for the benefit of St. Margaret's Hall, Brighton." Under that was the line, "Him that cometh to me I will in no wise cast out." Then was printed the six-stanza poem.

Invalid Charlotte Elliott read the poem. Tears welled in her eyes. Her memory went back to the day her minister-brother had organized a bazaar to start his school. She recalled too that everybody in town had helped. Everybody, that is, except her—a forty-six-year-old spinster who could hardly get about her room.

Lonely and helpless, Charlotte Elliott had written the poem to console other invalids. She had sent it to a publisher in the hope that from its sale she might contribute a few shillings to her brother's school. And now her poem was bringing in more revenue than all the bazaars the town could give.

Across the Atlantic, in Boston, a music teacher, composer, hymn-book publisher, and choir director named Lowell Mason was gathering religious poems and setting them to music. He encouraged his pupils to do likewise. One of Mason's pupils was an impoverished youth from York, Maine, named William Bradbury,

who hadn't seen an organ or piano until he was fourteen years old but who progressed so rapidly that he was soon directing music at the mammoth Baptist Tabernacle in New York City. He furthered his studies in Europe and was himself to edit and publish sixty hymnbooks.

The doctor was pleased with his call that day in 1834. He had left his patient so happy that she was crying. The little leaflet must have helped Charlotte Elliott's morale, for the following year she published a whole book of hymn-poems. She was to write many another during her long life of eighty-two years. Perhaps the good doctor might have wept a little himself had he known that it was his patient who had written the poem printed on the leaflet.

In later years Mr. Elliott said that his invalid sister did more good by writing one hymn than he had done during his "course of a long ministry."

It was in 1849, shortly after his return from Europe, that William Bradbury composed music that was set to Charlotte Elliott's poem.

> Just as I am, without one plea,
> But that Thy blood was shed for me,
> And that Thou bidd'st me come to Thee,
> O Lamb of God, I come! I come!

44. A Dying Actress Reads the Bible

To wave after wave of applause the curtain went down. A tall, beautiful actress with regular features walked off the stage of London's Richmond Theatre. That night in 1837 Sarah Adams made her last appearance as Lady Macbeth. When she was five years old her mother had died of tuberculosis. Her sister Eliza was bedridden with the disease. And now she herself was breaking at the age of thirty-two.

Her days on the stage over, Sarah Adams turned to writing lyric verse, dramatic poems, and hymns. She contributed articles to the religious periodical *The Repository*. For themes for her hymn-poems the former actress drew upon the Bible. One day in 1840, while reading the book of Genesis, Sarah Flower Adams pondered the story of Jacob at Bethel. Thus was born what has been called the greatest hymn ever written by a woman. The following year, with thirteen other hymns from her pen, it was published for the first time. Seven years later Sarah Adams died.

On September 19, 1901, churches in every city in America opened their doors. People stopped on city streets. Farmers stopped at their plows. Workmen stopped their machines. Some stood only in silent prayer for five minutes in reverence to the memory of the assassinated William McKinley. Others prayed aloud. Still others sang "Nearer, My God, to Thee." Just before the President had died he had said, "Nearer, my God, to Thee. . . . God's will be done."

A well-remembered story about the hymn concerns a fateful Sunday night in April, 1912, and the sinking of the luxury liner *Titanic*. As the few lifeboats with their cargo of six hundred pulled away, hope was lost for fifteen hundred helpless souls on the decks of the stricken ship. Some say it is tradition, but others say it is true that band leader Wallace Hartley struck up "Nearer, My God, to Thee" and that the singing of this hymn was hushed only by the freezing waves that closed over the sinking vessel.

Few works of even the most scholarly hymn writers have escaped alteration by critics and editors. Many a professional editor and learned scholar has tried his hand at "improving" the lines of "Nearer, My God, to Thee." Yet, word for word, line for line, the verses remain today just as the gifted woman of the theater wrote them. Add to such literary perfection so appealing a tune as only Lowell Mason could compose, and little wonder the result is a great hymn.

Nearer, my God, to Thee
Nearer to Thee!

E'en though it be a cross
That raiseth me;
Still all my song shall be,
Nearer, my God, to Thee!

45. A Hymn Is Written in a Stagecoach

But for the grinding wheels of his coach, the stage driver might have heard his lone passenger humming a familiar tune.

A few days earlier, Jemima Thompson had visited a school at Gray's Inn Road near London, where she had heard the children sing a Greek melody known as "Salamis." The air had made such an impression on her that she had searched every available hymnal for suitable words so that the children of her Sunday school class might sing it. But search as she would, Jemima Thompson could find no verses appropriate for the tune.

That was in the spring of 1841. Miss Thompson was twenty-eight years old. Besides writing for children's magazines, she taught a class of young girls at a London Congregational church where her father, Thomas Thompson, was superintendent of the Sunday school.

Humming the old Greek air while riding in the stagecoach, Jemima Thompson began fitting her own words to the melody. The trip was a short one —little more than an hour. But before the ride was ended Miss Thompson had two stanzas scribbled on the back of an envelope. Reaching home, she wrote copies for her class. Later

73

she added other stanzas to make a combination children's song and missionary hymn.

On the following Sunday superintendent Thompson heard the children of his daughter's class sing a song he had never heard before. "Where did that song come from?" he asked one of the children.

"Miss Jemima made it," was the reply.

Thomas Thompson was so delighted that he made a copy of Jemima's song and sent it, without his daughter's knowledge, to the *Sunday School Teachers Magazine.* From there it started on its way around the world.

Two years after she wrote her song, Jemima Thompson married Rev. Samuel Luke of the Congregational church in Bristol. Hence hymnbooks list the author as "Mrs. Jemima Luke." Mr. Luke died in 1868, but his widow lived to the age of ninety-three. She died in 1906.

Jemima Thompson Luke began her long writing career early in life. Her first story was published when she was only thirteen years old. And she wrote much. But Jemima Thompson Luke is remembered today for this hymn-poem, the first two stanzas of which she wrote on the back of an envelope while riding in a stagecoach.

I think when I read that sweet story of old
  When Jesus was here among men,
How He called little children as lambs to His fold,
  I should like to have been with them then.

I wish that His hand had been placed on my head,
  That His arm had been thrown around me;
And that I might have seen His kind look when He said,
  "Let the little ones come unto Me."

46. A Doctor of Divinity Delights in Doodling

Scotland's foremost hymn writer, Rev. Horatius Bonar, D.D., was forever doodling on envelopes and in note pads he carried in his pockets to jot down lines of hymns whenever they came to him. But Dr. Bonar's note pads were filled as much with caricatures and other sketches as they were with lines of poetry.

Dr. Bonar loved the hymns of Watts, Wesley, Cowper, and Newton; but his congregation at the Free Church of Scotland, in the town of Kelso, would not sing them. At a later charge, the huge Chalmers Memorial Church in Edinburgh, Bonar's efforts to depart from the custom of Psalm singing met with such opposition that some of his church officers walked out.

But the children weren't concerned with church customs. They cared little that the Presbyterian Church in Scotland was controlled by the government and that use of any songbook but the Psalter was forbidden.

To Horatius Bonar the adherence to church laws was of little significance. He lived his religion and preached the gospel as he saw it. A visitor once wrote of him: "His voice was low, quiet, and impressive. His prayer was as simple as a child's. Once he paused and addressed the Sunday school children who sat by themselves on one side of the pulpit. He is just like his hymns—not great, but tender, sweet, and tranquil."

Before delivering his sermon each Sunday, Dr. Bonar always visited the Sunday school and sang hymns with the children. Often he gave them printed leaflets of his own verse, and they sang the words to familiar music.

As editor of the *Quarterly Journal of Prophecy* Dr. Bonar published an original hymn in each issue for twenty-five years. Some critics said of his poems that they would hardly pass even as gospel hymns, but Bonar published them anyway.

In 1898 the United Presbyterian Church of Scotland published a hymnal of its own. It includes a liberal selection of Bonar's total output of more than six hundred hymn-poems. Here is one that Dr. Bonar wrote during the 1840's expressly for children of his Sunday school. If it is inferior, the critics have overlooked something, for not a word has been changed since Horatius Bonar scribbled the lines in one of his notebooks and doodled on the margins four incomplete faces and the head of a man wearing a hat.

> I heard the voice of Jesus say,
> "Come unto Me and rest;
> Lay down, thou weary one, lay down
> Thy head upon My breast."
> I came to Jesus as I was,
> Weary, and worn, and sad;
> I found in Him a restingplace,
> And He has made me glad.

47. A Sick Preacher Takes a Walk

During the first half of the last century it was a common occurrence for the townspeople of Brixham, England, to see a frail middle-aged man stroll thoughtfully by the seashore. The mild-mannered man was the town's parson. He had taken his daily walks by the sea for more than twenty years. That was the way he thought out many of his sermons. For there by the sea he daily talked with God.

On a Sunday afternoon in September, 1847, Rev. Henry Francis Lyte walked with a heavy heart. His steps were uncommonly slow.

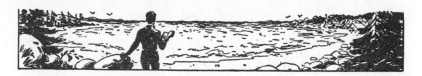

He knew that this was the last time he would tread the familiar path.

When he was thirty years old, Mr. Lyte had taken the little church at Brixham because he thought the salt air might help mend his health. Now, when he was fifty-four, his lung ailment had grown worse. Doctors said he would have to leave Brixham and go to the warmer climate of Italy.

At the morning service that Sunday in 1847 the ailing minister had administered his last sacrament. Now as he walked beside the sea for the last time he made notes for his farewell message to friends whose joys and sorrows he had shared for almost a quarter of a century.

In Italy he would be among strangers. But the gentle man knew there was one Friend who would go with him "in life, in death," no matter where he might go. And as he talked with God that Sunday afternoon, Mr. Lyte put his prayer on paper. He gave the paper to a relative, and the relative put it away in a trunk.

Henry Francis Lyte died in southern France two months after leaving Brixham. He never reached Italy.

Lyte's prayer-poem was published as a hymn. But in 1861 composer William Henry Monk was editing a hymnal in London when he decided that the music to "Abide with Me" was inferior to the beautifully written lines. A few feet away Monk's assistant banged away at a piano. But so engrossed was composer Monk that he was oblivious to the playing of Thalberg's "Fantasia" and, it is claimed, composed the music currently sung to "Abide with Me" in ten minutes. It was indeed a marked contrast to the solitude in which the words were composed by a dying preacher while he strolled for the last time by the sea, quietly communing with God.

> Abide with me; fast falls the eventide;
> The darkness deepens; Lord, with me abide:
> When other helpers fail, and comforts flee,
> Help of the helpless, O abide with me!

77

48. A Famous Carol Lies Unprinted for Four Years

Berkshire County is in western Massachusetts. Stretching along the Hoosic River in Berkshire County is a range of mountains known as the Berkshire Hills. On the lower edge of the Berkshire Hills is the village of Sandisfield. Across Massachusetts lies the town of Weston. Seven miles from Weston is the town of Wayland.

Few people living in these three towns have ever heard of a modest Unitarian minister named Edmund Hamilton Sears, who during his lifetime of sixty-six years lived in all three.

Dr. Sears was born in Sandisfield a century and a half ago. He spent most of his life serving a small church at Wayland. He died and was buried at Weston.

With a doctor's degree from Harvard, Edmund Hamilton Sears was equipped to fill a metropolitan pulpit. But he had grown up in the Berkshire Hills, and he loved the relaxed life of a small town. For there, removed from distractions of the city, he could write for the *Monthly Religious Magazine,* of which he was associate editor.

While a young minister of twenty-four, Sears wrote a Christmas hymn entitled "Calm on the Listening Ears of Night." That was in 1834. The number is rarely sung today.

Twelve years later the scholarly minister wrote another Christmas poem. But since his first Christmas poem had met with only mild success, he put his new poem in his desk, and there it lay for three years. Then, just before Christmas in 1849, Sears took the poem from his desk and, under the title "Peace on Earth," sent it to the publisher of Boston's *Christian Register*. It lay in the publisher's desk for another year. Finally, in 1850, Dr. Sears' poem was published.

Edmund Hamilton Sears lived quietly. He died quietly. Few people even in the small towns where he was born, ministered, and died have heard his name. All told, he wrote five books. They have been forgotten. He wrote hundreds of articles, poems, and hymns. They too have faded into oblivion.

But no sooner had "Peace on Earth" been published in the *Christian Register* than it was set to music by composer Richard S. Willis. And though both the author and a publisher friend had thought so little of it that it wasn't even printed for four years after it was written, it is found today in nearly every Christian hymnal around the world and has been called by critics one of the finest Christmas carols ever written.

> It came upon the midnight clear,
>   That glorious song of old,
> From angels bending near the earth,
>   To touch their harps of gold:
> "Peace on the earth, good will to men,"
>   From heaven's all-gracious King.
> The world in solemn stillness lay,
>   To hear the angels sing.

49. A Writer Discredits Her Most Lasting Piece of Work

A century ago a book had to be superb to have a sale of two hundred thousand copies. Elizabeth Payson Prentiss' *Stepping Heavenward* passed that mark. Her *The Flower of the Family* sold just short of that figure, and her collection of one-hundred twenty-three poems, under the title *Religious Poems,* also enjoyed a tremendous sale.

Elizabeth Payson Prentiss was one of the most prolific and best known religious writers of the last century. Born and reared in a pious and cultured atmosphere, the youngest daughter of Rev.

Edward Payson taught school in Portland, Maine (where she was born in 1818); Ipswich, Massachusetts; and Richmond, Virginia. Miss Payson married Presbyterian minister Dr. George L. Prentiss, quit teaching and, her frail health notwithstanding, wrote incessantly.

Writing was natural with the comely and petite Mrs. Prentiss. Perhaps that was why, when she was inspired to write a poem one day in 1856, the lines came to her as rapidly as she could put them on paper. But when she was into the third stanza, the work became laborious. The lines ceased to come. She put the unfinished poem away and dismissed it from her mind.

In 1869 Elizabeth Prentiss was looking through a stack of discarded papers when she came across the poem she had begun thirteen years before. Dr. Prentiss, then professor at New York's Union Theological Seminary, insisted that the poem be finished. Mrs. Prentiss didn't think very highly of the verses, but to please her husband, she completed the third stanza and added a fourth.

Dr. Prentiss had copies of the poem printed for distribution among their friends. Someone sent one of the leaflets to composer William Howard Doane in Cincinnati. Doane set the verses to music and published them in his songbook, *Songs of Devotion*. The new hymn became immediately popular in the great revivals of the 1870's. It has been a favorite ever since.

Though exceedingly popular during the last half of the past century, the works of Elizabeth Payson Prentiss have, for the most part, been forgotten. But the one poem she regarded as being inferior to all the rest has outlived everything else she wrote. It was sung at her funeral in 1878.

> More love to Thee, O Christ,
> More love to Thee!
> Hear Thou the prayer I make
> On bended knee;

This is my earnest plea:
More love, O Christ, to Thee,
More love to Thee! More love to Thee!

50. The Author of Eighty-five Books Is Remembered for a Single Poem

During the week days Rev. Sabine Baring-Gould ministered to his little congregation in the mill town of Horbury, England. On Sundays he converted his bachelor quarters into a church. At night he held school in the same room. After classes he retired to his upstairs bedroom and wrote into the small hours of morning.

Whitmonday was a time-honored day of festival for the children of Horbury. It was the custom for them to march, with crosses and banners, to neighboring towns where they joined other children for the annual celebration.

For the event, in 1864, Mr. Baring-Gould was asked to escort the group. On the night before the processional the youthful Anglican minister searched hymnals in vain for a Christian song the children might sing as they marched. Giving up the search, he wrote some verses of his own. Over them he wrote the title "Hymn for Procession with Cross and Banners." Baring-Gould had no thought of writing a hymn. Indeed, he said years later, he had no idea that his hastily written poem might ever be published.

The same year he wrote his marching song for children, Baring-Gould chanced to rescue a mill worker's daughter from drowning. He fell in love with her, sent her away to school, and married her in 1868. At the death of his father in 1881 he inherited a fortune and moved into a mansion at Lew Trenchard.

For fifty-two years Sabine Baring-Gould wrote a novel every year. He wrote books on religion. He wrote books on mythology, biography, travel, folklore, and theology. He published a complete book of hymns. His *Lives of the Saints* alone fills fifteen volumes.

Had Baring-Gould lived twenty-six days longer he would have been ninety years old when he died in 1924. It is said that the literary catalog of the British Museum lists more titles by him than by any other writer of the Victorian era. But as prolific as he was, Sabine Baring-Gould is best remembered today for a poem he wrote in less than an hour one night when he was thirty years old.

Part of the credit for the popularity of the poem must be given to a youthful organist who was later to carve a niche for himself in the world of music. For the composer who set the poem to music was Sir Arthur Sullivan.

> Onward, Christian soldiers,
>   Marching as to war,
> With the cross of Jesus
>   Going on before!
> Christ, the royal Master,
>   Leads against the foe;
> Forward into battle,
>   See, His banner go!

51. A Youthful Writer Inspires a Scholar

It was a trait of Baptist minister A. J. Gordon to hum snatches of original music while he worked. When he caught an air that pleased him, he would have a member of his family play the notes on the piano. If they offered promise as the nucleus of a melody, he would jot them down and build a tune around them.

One day in 1864 Dr. Gordon was humming as he mused over an old English hymnbook, the *London Hymnal*. On one of the pages was a hymn which struck him as being superbly written. There was no name of the author. But whoever the poet, the lines were so beautifully written that Dr. Gordon thought the music fell short of doing them justice.

Adoniram Judson Gordon, D.D., named for the pioneer Baptist missionary, was born in New Hampshire on April 19, 1836. He was educated at Brown University and Newton Theological Seminary. Ordained at twenty-seven, he became pastor of a Baptist church at Jamaica Plains, Massachusetts. Dr. Gordon later went to Clarendon Street Baptist Church, Boston, and died in 1895 at the height of his notable career.

It was while gathering material for one of his hymnbooks that Dr. Gordon was inspired by words of the hymn "My Jesus, I Love Thee" in the *London Hymnal*. Moved by the beauty of the lines, he resolved to compose a tune appropriate to the sentiment of the poem. Finally striking an air that suited him, the minister-composer wrote a tune for the hymn that has made it a favorite of Protestant denominations the world over.

For almost a century "My Jesus, I Love Thee" has been included in hymnals with the stately works of Wesley, Watts, Cowper, and Heber. And the lines that so inspired Dr. Gordon have withstood the most critical editing.

Only in recent years has the name of the anonymous author become known. Certainly Dr. Gordon would have been surprised to have known the writer's identity. His name was William Ralf Featherstone. The hymn was written shortly after his conversion in Toronto in 1858.

William Ralf Featherstone died in the prime of life at the age of

thirty-six—twenty years after writing his inspiring hymn-poem. And that deduction is what would have interested Dr. Gordon. For the hymn that the scholarly minister had regarded as a masterpiece was written by a sixteen-year-old Canadian boy.

> My Jesus, I love Thee, I know Thou art mine,
> For Thee all the follies of sin I resign;
> My precious Redeemer, my Saviour art Thou;
> If ever I loved Thee, my Jesus, 'tis now.

52. A Hymn Is Born of a Fatal Accident

"The work of God in Philadelphia" is what men called the great city-wide revival campaign of 1858. Every Protestant denomination in the city joined in the mammoth movement. Services were held morning and evening in churches, convention halls, and even theaters. Ministers and laymen came from all parts of the nation. For this was the forerunner of the great revival campaigns of the latter half of the last century.

Few veteran preachers were more powerful in the movement than was youthful twenty-nine-year-old Episcopalian Dudley Tyng. Tyng was a born preacher, and he had been tutored by his minister-father. One Sunday during the campaign he stood before five thousand men in Philadelphia's Jayne's Hall. Before he pronounced the benediction, one out of every five men in the congregation was on his knees in prayer.

On the following Wednesday Tyng was at work in his study. For relaxation he went to a nearby barn to watch workmen operate a corn-shelling apparatus. When he thoughtlessly moved too close to the machinery, a sleeve of his coat caught in a moving cog, and his arm was literally torn from his shoulder.

Doctors and a score of ministers gathered at the bedside. The dying Mr. Tyng tried to sing "Rock of Ages," but he was too weak.

84

The young man's father, Rev. Stephen H. Tyng, leaned close to hear the last words of his son who had so recently brought thousands to their knees. "Tell them," was the faint whisper, "to stand up for Jesus."

The phrase so impressed Presbyterian minister George Duffield, Jr., that his next sermon was from the text, "Stand, therefore, having your loins girt about with truth . . . ." For the conclusion of his dramatic sermon Mr. Duffield read a poem he had written. A member of the congregation had the verses printed on leaflets for use in the Sunday school. Someone sent one of the leaflets, without Duffield's knowledge, to a Baptist periodical.

Thirty years earlier composer George James Webb had written a secular song entitled " 'Tis Dawn, the Lark Is Singing." Webb's music had been adapted to the hymn "The Morning Light Is Breaking" and had become one of the most widely sung compositions of the time.

In 1864 Mr. Duffield was visiting Union army camps when he heard the soldiers singing the poem he had written—to the music of "The Morning Light Is Breaking." Until then he didn't even know he had written a hymn—a hymn that had been inspired six years earlier by the last words of a dying minister.

> Stand up, stand up for Jesus,
>   Ye soldiers of the cross;
> Lift high His royal banner,
>   It must not suffer loss:
> From vict'ry unto vict'ry
>   His army shall He lead,
> Till ev'ry foe is vanquished,
>   And Christ is Lord indeed.

53. A Gust of Wind Blows Down a Chimney

"The little things are infinitely the most important," once said British novelist Sir Arthur Conan Doyle. When one considers seemingly insignificant events that have led to the downfall of nations, little things that have changed the course of history, and trivial incidents that have made marked alterations in the lives of men, the gravity of Doyle's statement becomes obvious.

One day in 1858 a frail young woman sat in an art gallery in Germany. Her name was Frances Ridley Havergal. Since she was too delicate of health to attend school regularly, Miss Havergal's father had sought to make up the difference by encouraging travel during her sporadic class work. Hence she was visiting with friends in Dusseldorf.

It was purely by chance that Frances Havergal paused for a rest in the art gallery in front of a painting of Christ on the cross. Over the wreath of thorns she read the wording: "This have I done for thee; What hast thou done for me?"

Incidentally, it was this same painting and this same wording that changed the course of a sight-seeing tour for Count Nicolaus Ludwig Zinzendorf and thus altered the course of the world's religious history.

Inspired by the painting, Miss Havergal wrote a few lines of poetry. That night at the home of her hosts she pondered the lines and concluded that they were ill written. She tossed the paper into the fire. Then followed a simple incident that was to change her entire life. A gust of wind blew the paper back out onto the hearth.

Back in England, Miss Havergal showed the verses to her father, Rev. W. H. Havergal, a hymn writer and composer in his own

right. He encouraged Frances to add more stanzas to make her poem complete. And thus began one of the most brilliant careers in hymnology.

This remarkable woman wrote, in addition to hundreds of hymns, an entire volume of poetry. She learned French, Greek, German, Hebrew, and Latin. She could read both the Old and the New Testaments in the original. She memorized the entire New Testament, the Psalms, and the book of Isaiah. She became also an excellent soloist and pianist and composed several hymn tunes.

Frances Ridley Havergal died at the age of forty-three. When told that the end was near, she said, "Splendid! To be so near the gates of heaven!"

Many of her hymns are still in use around the world. In addition to the one given here, her "Take My Life and Let It Be" and "True Hearted, Whole Hearted" are equally popular. Below is the hymn that was inspired by the painting at the art gallery in Dusseldorf— but which would have been lost to the world had not a gust of air blown down a chimney in Germany a century ago.

> I gave my life for thee,
> My precious blood I shed,
> That thou might'st ransomed be,
> And quickened from the dead;
> I gave, I gave my life for thee,
> What hast thou giv'n for Me?

54. Composers Due Credit for Success of Many Hymns

"I have seen vast audiences melted by a simple hymn," once wrote evangelistic singer Ira David Sankey.

Actually, few people think of the meaning of the words when they sing a hymn along with others in a congregation. This is unfortunate. For while some hymn-poems are little more than lines

that rhyme, others represent some of the finest poetry ever written. But regardless of their literary and inspirational value, many hymns that otherwise might have enjoyed only mild success or even been lost entirely have been made immortal by the work of those little-known artisans of the keyboard—the composers who wrote the music.

The church owes an everlasting debt of gratitude to composer Lowell Mason, who devoted his talents and boundless energy to the cause of religious music. Many an audience has "melted" to Mason's music for "Nearer, My God, to Thee," "My Faith Looks Up to Thee," and "There Is a Fountain Filled with Blood."

Lowell Mason taught and encouraged many a promising beginner. One of the most notable of Mason's proteges was William Bradbury. Bradbury in turn encouraged blind Fanny Crosby to turn her talents from writing secular songs to hymns for the church. Following Mason's example, Bradbury organized and taught rural "singing schools." A product of such a school was poverty-stricken Philip Bliss, who was later to write both words and music for "Almost Persuaded," "Wonderful Words of Life," and "Let the Lower Lights Be Burning." And William Bradbury, poverty-stricken himself in his youth, contributed immortal music to such hymn-poems as "Just As I Am," "Sweet Hour of Prayer," and "He Leadeth Me."

And so, while homage is paid the poet, no less tribute is due the noble composers who have helped make immortal the lines of many a poet.

It was in 1859 that William Bradbury came upon the following unsigned poem. Some believe it might have been written by Rev. Henry F. Lyte, author of "Abide with Me." Others attribute it to Dorothy Ann Thrupp, in whose book it first appeared. Some hymnals publish the song with no name of the author. But whoever the poet, it was William Batchelder Bradbury who set the words to music and gave the Christian world another great hymn before he worked himself to death at the age of fifty-two.

88

Saviour, like a shepherd lead us,
    Much we need Thy tender care;
In Thy pleasant pastures feed us,
    For our use Thy folds prepare:
Blessed Jesus, blessed Jesus,
    Thou hast bought us, Thine we are;
Blessed Jesus, blessed Jesus,
    Thou hast bought us, Thine we are.

55. A Southern Tune Becomes the Marching Song of the North

To pass time around the firehouses, the firemen of Richmond, Virginia, sang everything in the songbooks—and some things that weren't in the books. Then in 1855 a local musician named John W. Staffe wrote a tune just for the firemen to sing. But Staffe left for his firemen friends the problem of finding words to go with the tune he had written for them.

The tune swept out of the firehouses of Richmond like a prairie holocaust. In less time than it takes to hitch a team to a fire truck everybody was singing John Staffe's tune—to everybody's lyrics. The lilting melody was taken up even at camp meetings and sung to words of age-old hymns.

In 1859 a popular topic of conversation was the hanging of John Brown, the self-styled abolitionist who, with help of his sons, sought to free all the slaves in America. But John Brown wound up in-

stead at the end of a rope. "John Brown" became a byword. His earthly remains were hardly returned to the soil when his name became associated with the firehouse tune. In the South people sang "They hanged John Brown to a sour apple tree," "John Brown's baby had a cold upon its chest," and any other "John Brown" phrase that met the fancy of the vocalist. In the North they sang, to the same music, about hanging Jeff Davis to the same species of tree.

In 1861 Boston's gifted writer Julia Ward Howe rode as a guest of President Lincoln through Union Army camps along the Potomac. Every soldier in the Federal Army seemed to be singing about hanging Confederate President Jefferson Davis to a sour apple tree. And the enthusiastic Yankees added a lusty "Glory, hallelujah!"

The tune was ringing in Julia Ward Howe's ears when she retired to her Washington hotel. She tried to sleep, but still she heard the lilting tune. A splendid bit of music this was, but how silly the words! Finally, she got up from her bed and, still in her night robe, wrote some verses of her own. The Union Army took them up as its marching song to music written by a Southerner for his friends to sing while passing time at the firehouses of Richmond.

Ironically, after Jefferson Davis had fled from Richmond, the Union Army marched into the city singing Julia Ward Howe's words to the tune written by John W. Staffe of Richmond.

> Mine eyes have seen the glory
>   Of the coming of the Lord;
> He is trampling out the vintage
>   Where the grapes of wrath are stored;
> He hath loosed the fateful lightning
>   Of His terrible swift sword;
> His truth is marching on.
>   Glory! glory, hallelujah!
> Our God is marching on.

56. A Governor's Son Discovers a Hymn He Wrote

In the spring of 1865 a thirty-one-year-old minister took his place in the pulpit of the Second Baptist Church at Rochester, New York. As he waited to deliver his trial sermon before the new congregation, he thumbed through a hymnal to select an impressive song. Musing through the book, Rev. Joseph H. Gilmore's thumb stopped on one of the pages. His eyes widened. Then he smiled. His thoughts went back to a night three years earlier.

The night Dr. Gilmore recalled was that of March 26, 1862. The War Between the States had swung into its tragic stride. Abraham Lincoln had not yet issued his Emancipation Proclamation, and it seemed that nobody on either side knew what the bloodshed was about. Nor was there any indication of when the struggle might end. Everywhere people were praying for divine guidance. In Philadelphia, Joseph Henry Gilmore, D.D., son of the governor of New Hampshire, delivered an inspiring message on Psalm 23 to a group gathered for prayer at the First Baptist Church.

After the prayer service, Dr. Gilmore and his wife went to the home of deacon Thomas Wattson for the night. The deacon complimented Gilmore on the selection of his text and his inspiring message. The more Dr. Gilmore thought on the subject, the more he became, as he later wrote, "impressed with the blessedness of being led by God."

In recalling the occasion Dr. Gilmore further related that "the blessedness of God's leadership so grew upon me that I took out my pencil, wrote the hymn just as it stands today, handed it to my wife, and thought no more of it."

And that is why Joseph H. Gilmore's eyes widened in the pulpit

at Rochester three years later. Though he had forgotten his poem, Mrs. Gilmore had not. Without her husband's knowledge, she had sent the poem to the religious periodical *Watchman and Reflector*. Though it was published shortly thereafter, it had not come to Dr. Gilmore's attention, and he did not realize he had written a hymn-poem until he opened the book at "He Leadeth Me." "That was the first time I knew that my hymn had found a place among the songs of the church. I shall never forget the impression made upon me," he added, "by coming in contact then and there with my own assertion of God's blessed leadership."

Though Dr. Gilmore had forgotten his poem and had indeed never seen it in print before he found it in a hymnbook, it might still have been lost but for the alertness of a composer. For it was William Bradbury who discovered its merits as a hymn, set it to music, and published it in *The Golden Censer* in 1864. It is Bradbury's music that has assured the immortality of "He Leadeth Me."

> He leadeth me! O blessed tho't!
>   O words with heav'nly comfort fraught!
> Whate'er I do, where'er I be,
>   Still 'tis God's hand that leadeth me!

> REFRAIN:
> He leadeth me, He leadeth me,
>   By His own hand He leadeth me:
> His faithful follow'r I would be,
>   For by His hand He leadeth me.

57. A Hymn Is Born of an Epidemic

People were dying all over New York City. An epidemic was claiming an appalling toll. When Rev. Robert Lowry was not visiting sick members of his Hanson Place Baptist Church,

he was burying those who had crossed over Jordan. One hot day in July, 1864, the thirty-eight-year-old clergyman was near collapse. He fell exhausted on a couch in his Brooklyn home. As he lay there, he began recounting the friends he had buried and thought of others for whom there was little hope. Then his thoughts drifted to the great reunion at the river of life. Soon he was busy writing a hymn.

Robert Lowry, D.D., was one of those rare individuals to whom God entrusts many talents. He was an educator, a gifted orator, an administrator, a poet, musician, and a preacher. At middle age he seriously took up the study of music and composed some of the finest of hymn tunes for his own poems as well as for those of other writers.

But with all his talents, Robert Lowry claimed to be only a preacher. After his hymns had made him famous and he was a composer, he said he felt "a sort of meanness." Preaching, he insisted, was his profession. Hymn writing was an avocation. And he said he would prefer preaching a gospel sermon to an attentive congregation to writing any time. When asked what sort of method he used when composing music for his hymn-poems, Lowry insisted that he had no method. He said music simply ran through his head all the time, and when the mood struck him, he merely jotted down the notes on any suitable material at hand—the back of an envelope, the edge of a newspaper, or in a notebook. As for the words, they too came by inspiration; Lowry claimed to have written verse only when in the proper mood.

One would judge that preacher Robert Lowry must have had lots of inspiration and moods before he died at Plainfield, New Jersey, in 1899. For his name appears over many of the most popular Christian songs. Who hasn't heard "Where Is My Wandering Boy Tonight?" which Lowry wrote in 1877 for the temperance movement? What revival campaign or camp meeting hasn't included the singing of Lowry's music to "Nothing but the Blood"?

Exhausted as Rev. Lowry might have been, his mood was in good trim that sultry afternoon in 1864. Reaching for a scrap of paper, he wrote the following verses. Then he went over to his organ and composed for them a tune that is familiar to churchgoers from the Atlantic to the Pacific.

However he might have loved preaching, Robert Lowry underestimated his talents. His sermons reached thousands. But his hymns have moved and inspired millions for nearly a century. His preaching has been forgotten. His hymns live on. Here is one of his first, inspired by the thought of a happy reunion of friends he had buried during an epidemic in New York.

> Shall we gather at the river,
>   Where bright angel feet have trod;
> With its crystal tide forever
>   Flowing by the throne of God?

> REFRAIN:
> Yes, we'll gather at the river,
>   The beautiful, the beautiful river;
> Gather with the saints at the river
>   That flows by the throne of God.

58. A Choir Singer Writes While a Minister Prays

Hymns have been written under strange circumstances. They have been written aboard ships, on trains, in railway stations, on busy streets, at deathbeds, by the sea, and in the quiet of scholarly libraries. Isaac Watts did much of his writing under a shade tree. Charles Wesley often wrote while riding horseback. John Wesley wrote while riding in his buggy. Fanny Crosby dictated verse wherever she was. John B. Dykes composed music while walking. Some hymns are sung to music originally composed for secular songs. And many a hymn tune was composed a century or more before or after the verse was written.

John T. Grape lived in Baltimore. He played the organ at a

Methodist church there. Grape made no claim to being a composer but modestly said he loved to "dabble" at writing music.

Mrs. Elvina M. Hall also lived in Baltimore. She sang in the choir at the Methodist church where John T. Grape played the organ. Mrs. Hall made no claim to being a poet but occasionally tried her hand at writing verse.

One day in 1865 organist Grape was dabbling at writing music when he came up with a tune that he thought might have merit. He didn't bother to send his composition to a publisher. Instead, he handed it to his pastor, Rev. Schrick, and gave it no more thought.

One Sunday morning in 1865, Mrs. Elvina Hall was sitting in the choir loft of the church in Baltimore when Mr. Schrick began offering a prayer of the old-fashioned variety that gives little promise of having an ending. While Mr. Schrick prayed, Mrs. Hall thumbed through her songbook, *The New Lute of Zion*. Mr. Schrick prayed on. Mrs. Hall began scribbling on the flyleaf of *The New Lute of Zion*. Schrick prayed on. Mrs. Hall turned from scribbling to writing verse. By the time Mr. Schrick said amen, Mrs. Hall had written a four-stanza poem.

Like organist Grape, Mrs. Hall gave her poem to Mr. Schrick. It is doubtful, however, that she divulged to the good minister the circumstances under which she had written it. At any rate, when Mr. Schrick read the poem, he recognized that the lines fitted the music organist Grape had given him some days earlier.

Hymns have been written under divers circumstances. While most might have been written under more orthodox conditions and few have been set to music in so unique a manner, many a conventionally composed hymn fails to enjoy the popularity of this one which was written in a songbook while a minister prayed.

> I hear the Saviour say,
>   "Thy strength indeed is small,
> Child of weakness, watch and pray,
>   Find in Me thine all in all."

59. A Barefoot Boy Goes Peddling

One day in 1848 a ragged, barefoot boy just past ten years old walked a dusty backwoods road into the town of Rome, Pennsylvania. The lad had come from his rural log-cabin home in Clearfield County to sell a basket of berries he had picked from the swamps. He wanted to add a few pennies to those he had been saving to buy a cheap violin.

The only musical instrument the lad had ever heard was a flute his father had whittled for him from a cane. But while walking the streets in search of a market for his berries, the boy heard strains of piano music. He knew it must be a piano because his mother had told him of the sound. The lad ventured to the house from which the sound came and shyly put his basket on the porch. Silently he stood at the open door.

When the lady of the house saw the uninvited visitor, she abruptly stopped playing. The lad begged her to please play some more. Instead, she ordered the young peddler away and scolded him for making tracks on her porch.

Such was the early life of Philip Bliss. Two decades later his name was a household word wherever people sang gospel music. A tall,

96

handsome six-footer with a winning personality and genial manner, he had a rich baritone voice which carried him to the pinnacle of evangelistic singing. As a soloist, Philip Bliss was sought out by revival leaders of his time, including the great Dwight L. Moody. He wrote his own words and composed his own music. But for his untimely death in a train wreck at the age of thirty-eight, Philip Bliss might have become the greatest of all composer-singers of Christian songs. For he sang them masterfully, and he wrote them rapidly.

One night Bliss sat back to listen to evangelist Moody tell of a shipwreck on Lake Erie, just off the harbor at Cleveland, because the lower lights along the coast had gone out. "The Master will take care of the great light," said Moody in referring to the main lighthouse, "but let us keep the lower lights burning."

The following night Philip Bliss sang a new hymn for which he had written both words and music. It is found in hymnals around the world today. The title is "Let the Lower Lights Be Burning."

While he was singing for evangelist D. W. Whittle in Chicago, during an evening service Philip Bliss pondered the thought that most hymns are written around the theme of man's love for God. The following morning, while waiting for his wife to call breakfast, Philip Bliss reversed the theme and wrote:

> I am so glad that our Father in heav'n
> Tells of His love in the Book He has giv'n;
> Wonderful things in the Bible I see;
> This is the dearest, that Jesus loves me.

During his short career Philip Bliss earned more than thirty thousand dollars in royalties alone. But remembering the poverty of his youth, he gave all but a modest livelihood to worthy causes. Here is another Christian song written by a genius who was so poor in his youth that he was denied the simple luxury of hearing a lady play her piano.

> Sing them over again to me,
> Wonderful words of life;
> Let me more of their beauty see,
> Wonderful words of life;

97

Words of life and beauty,
Teach me faith and duty:
Beautiful words, wonderful words,
Wonderful words of life.

60. ". . . God Kindly Veils My Eyes"

The night of December 29, 1876, marks one of the most tragic wrecks in the history of American railroading. For on that bitter cold night a west-bound express train crashed through a trestle over a swollen stream near Ashtabula, Ohio, caught fire, and carried a hundred passengers to a burning death. On board the ill-fated Chicago-bound train was Philip Bliss, beloved and famous gospel song composer and singer.

Born in rural Pennsylvania, Philip Bliss was reared in abject poverty. In his teens he worked at a country sawmill for ten dollars a month and attended a singing school conducted by William Bradbury. As Lowell Mason had encouraged Bradbury, Bradbury encouraged Philip Bliss.

In his early twenties he married, bought a ramshackle buggy and a horse he named "Fanny," and went about the countryside with his wife, teaching music. His average income was thirteen dollars a month.

At twenty-six Bliss wrote a secular song he called "Lora Vale." Having learned his first notes on a homemade flute whittled from a cane, he sent his song to the Chicago firm of Root & Cady, music publishers, with the request that if his composition were acceptable, he would appreciate a real flute in exchange. Reading the manuscript, big-hearted composer George Frederick Root sent Bliss the finest flute he could find, along with a note that a job with the firm of Root & Cady was waiting for him if he wanted to come to Chicago.

At thirty-two Philip Bliss was director of music at Chicago's First Congregational Church, editor of hymnals for Root & Cady, and

fast becoming a great singer of gospel music. And by 1872 penitents by the thousands were walking the sawdust trail to his solos.

Composing both words and music for his gospel songs, Bliss was ever alert for themes. His "Hold the Fort" was written after hearing evangelist D. W. Whittle relate a dramatic story of how outnumbered Federals at Altoona Pass were given hope by a signaled message from General W. T. Sherman in 1864.

One Sunday night, while waiting for a train in Ohio, Bliss slipped into a church and took a rear seat. The minister, a Mr. Brundage, was reading from the Acts of the Apostles: "Then Agrippa said unto Paul, 'Almost thou persuadest me to be a Christian.'" During his sermon Mr. Brundage said, "To be almost saved is to be entirely lost." And Philip Bliss had the theme for one of his famous gospel songs.

After spending Christmas with his mother in Pennsylvania, Bliss and his wife were returning to Chicago when their train plunged through the trestle. The powerful singer tore his way from the burning cars. Unable to find his wife, he fought his way back through the flames. In a vain effort to save her, he died at her side. His trunk was salvaged, and in it evangelist Whittle found an unfinished hymn. It began: "I know not what awaits me, God kindly veils my eyes."

Here is the hymn Philip Bliss wrote after hearing a sermon while waiting for a train.

> "Almost persuaded" now to believe;
>   "Almost persuaded" Christ to reccive;
> Seems now some soul to say,
>   "Go, Spirit, go Thy way,
> Some more convenient day,
>   On Thee I'll call."

61. A Hymn Is Born of a Casual Remark

Joseph Philbrick Webster was an accomplished musician. In addition to playing the violin and other instruments, he was also a prolific composer of secular songs. In the East, where he was born in 1819, Webster had been an active member of the Handel and Haydn Society. In his early thirties, like many another young man of his time, he migrated westward to Indiana. In 1857 he moved further west and settled at Elkhorn, Wisconsin.

Sanford Fillmore Bennett was a general practitioner of medicine. In 1861 Dr. Bennett also settled at Elkhorn and set up practice there. And like many another professional man, physician Bennett had a hobby. Bennett's hobby was writing verse.

Shortly after the verse-writing Dr. Bennett hung out his shingle at Elkhorn, he and composer Webster struck up a partnership in the production of secular songs—the physician writing the lyrics and Webster supplying the music. But with his medical practice, Dr. Bennett apparently was unable to supply words enough to keep his musician friend in steady employment. This one-sided production resulted in periods of idleness for Webster, who, being somewhat temperamental, suffered spells of melancholia. These spells of idleness were usually spent in the comforts of Bennett's office near his pot-bellied stove.

One autumn day in 1867 composer Webster sauntered into Dr. Bennett's office and hung his hat and his violin on the usual hook but said nothing. The silence that followed was indication enough to physician Bennett that his collaborator was suffering one of his dejected moods.

"What's the trouble now?" Bennett asked.

"Oh, nothing," Webster said somberly. "Everything will be all right by and by."

Turning back to his desk, where he wrote both prescriptions and verse, Bennett mused, " 'By and by.' That sweet by and by."

Dr. Bennett paused. He looked wonderingly at Webster. He reached for his pencil and writing paper. In that chance remark lay the theme for a song—not a secular number but a hymn.

While the inspired physician wrote rapidly at his desk, two townsmen joined Webster at the stove. Before half an hour had passed, Dr. Bennett handed his friend Webster three stanzas and a chorus. The sentiment of the verses so struck the musician that the melody came from his violin almost spontaneously. In less time than it had taken Bennett to write the words, Webster had his tune.

With the two townsmen, the physician and the composer formed a quartette and sang the new hymn within an hour after Webster had made his casual remark.

> There's a land that is fairer than day,
>   And by faith we can see it afar;
> For the Father waits over the way
>   To prepare us a dwelling place there.
>
> REFRAIN:
> In the sweet by and by,
>   We shall meet on that beautiful shore;
> In the sweet by and by,
>   We shall meet on that beautiful shore.

62. A Giant Plays at Dolls with Children

Phillips Brooks was a big preacher. Physically, mentally, and spiritually he was one of the biggest preachers in

America. The massive Episcopal minister stood six feet, six inches tall. He sang two hundred hymns from memory. He rolled out his powerful sermons at the rate of 250 words a minute. His writings raised the eyebrows of many a staid theologian. But his study —the study where the eloquent preacher-author outlined his scholarly sermons—was strewed with toys and dolls for his little friends, with whom he was never too busy to romp and play.

In December, 1868, the massive preacher walked the study of his Protestant Episcopal Church in Philadelphia. It was just before Christmas. He was outlining a sermon on the Nativity. Out in the church, Sunday school superintendent and organist Lewis Redner ran over music for the Yule services. Redner was a bachelor, but he loved children so much that largely through his efforts the Sunday school enrolment was increased from thirty-six members to more than a thousand.

But Lewis Redner could have loved children no more than did big Phillips Brooks. Three years earlier Dr. Brooks had visited the Holy Land, where he devoted most of his time to writing letters to his little friends back home about Bethlehem and the shepherds who watched their sheep just as they did when the Baby Jesus was born.

Carried away with vivid memories of the Holy Land, Phillips Brooks put aside work on his sermon and wrote a Christmas carol for the children of his Sunday school. He asked Lewis Redner to compose a tune for the verses. Day after day Redner carried the poem in his pocket. Then, on the night before Christmas, he awoke to strains of a melody which, he said, seemed to "come down from heaven." He got up out of bed and wrote the notes down. That Christmas morning in 1868 children of Philadelphia's Holy Trinity Church sang "O Little Town of Bethlehem" for the first time.

Dr. Phillips Brooks was made Protestant Episcopal Bishop of Massachusetts in 1891. Two years later, at the age of fifty-seven, he died in Boston. Historians call him a great preacher, dynamic and elegant. Writers have referred to him as having a "majestic face," "a massive frame," and a "princely form towering . . . as a giant." But a five-year-old girl best summed up his personality. Inquisitive as to why she did not see her big friend any more, the little girl was told that Dr. Brooks had gone to heaven. At that, the child said, though tears had begun to show in her eyes, "How happy the angels will be."

Here is the carol Phillips Brooks, who, like organist Lewis Redner, was a bachelor and had no children, wrote for his little friends to sing on Christmas in 1868.

> O little town of Bethlehem,
> How still we see thee lie!
> Above thy deep and dreamless sleep
> The silent stars go by;
> Yet in thy dark streets shineth
> The everlasting Light;
> The hopes and fears of all the years
> Are met in thee tonight.

63. A Mother Writes at the Bedside of Her Child

In his youth Frederick William Faber was a Protestant. But following the example of his friend John Henry Newman, at the age of thirty-one Faber changed to the Roman Catholic faith.

Becoming a priest in the Roman Church, Faber missed the hymns of Wesley, Watts, Newton, and others of the Protestant church. So Father Faber set about with his own pen to fill the void. And with certain appropriate editorial alterations, many of Roman Catholic priest Frederick W. Faber's hymns are sung today in Protestant churches around the world.

While Father Frederick Faber was writing "Faith of Our Fathers," "Hark, Hark, My Soul," and 148 other hymns a century ago, a young Englishwoman named Mary Ann Faulkner migrated to Philadelphia and married Protestant Episcopalian John Thomson, a member of the Free Public Library staff in the Quaker City.

One night in 1868 Mary Ann Thomson sat at the bedside of her typhoid-stricken son. While the child slept, Mrs. Thomson fell to humming familiar hymns. Among her favorites was Father Faber's "Hark, hark, my soul! angelic songs are swelling . . ."

Mary Ann Thomson was especially fond of the music of Faber's hymn. It had been composed by blind organist Henry Smart, and she thought it an excellent air for a missionary hymn. Having already written a number of hymn-poems, Mrs. Thomson set about writing some verses of her own to fit Henry Smart's music. She said that the verses came with little effort. But at the moment unable to write a suitable refrain, she put the poem aside. Three years passed before she found time from her household chores to write the simple refrain.

Strange things have happened in the birth of some hymns. Though a student of composer Henry Smart, organist James Walch didn't like the music Smart had written for Faber's hymn—the very tune Mrs. Thomson had liked so well. So Walch wrote a tune of his own for the same hymn. Then, after reading Mrs. Thomson's poem, a hymnal editor observed that the tune Walch had written was a natural mate for the verses. Thus the two were brought together, and "O Zion, Haste," Mary Ann Thomson's missionary hymn, is never sung to the music that inspired its writing. Instead, it is sung to the tune written to supplant the original tune.

Here is one stanza of the poem Mary Ann Thomson wrote at the bedside of her sick child in 1868. As mentioned, the refrain came three years later.

> O Zion, haste, thy mission, high fulfilling,
>   To tell to all the world that God is Light;

That He who made all nations is not willing
One soul should perish, lost in shades of night.

Publish glad tidings,
  Tidings of peace,
Tidings of Jesus,
  Redemption and release.

64. A Carpenter and the Lord Write a Hymn Together

On October 10, 1886, a pall of grief fell over the community of Lake Rice, Canada. The body of one of the town's best-loved citizens had been found in a small stream of water. The man's name was Joseph Scriven. He was sixty-six years old. For forty years Joseph Scriven had lived in and around Lake Rice, first with one family, then with another. He lived around among his friends, for Joseph Scriven didn't have a home of his own. When his body was found in the water-run, those who knew him best—the poor people of Lake Rice—wondered if the melancholy bachelor might have taken his life. They knew that forty years before, Joseph Scriven's sweetheart had accidentally drowned the day before their wedding and that Scriven had never overcome the shock.

Joseph Scriven was born in Dublin, Ireland, in 1820. He was educated on the Emerald Isle and graduated from Dublin's Trinity College. Scriven's life lay before him. He was engaged to a beautiful Irish lass. Then tragedy struck. The day before the wedding Scriven's

bride-to-be was accidentally drowned. When her body was taken from the pool, Joseph Scriven suffered a shock that was to go with him the rest of his life.

At the age of twenty-five Scriven migrated to Canada in the hope of forgetting. But he never forgot. Ten years later Scriven's mother fell ill of grief, and he wrote a poem to comfort her. He called it "What a Friend We Have in Jesus."

For forty years the grief-stricken Irishman, for whom life had once held so much, associated himself with the underprivileged and poor of Lake Rice and Port Hope, Canada. It is said that he gave even his clothes to those less fortunate than he. He sought out orphans whom he might help. He sawed wood and did patch carpentry for widows. But he never hired out to work for those able to pay. Some said he was eccentric. Some branded him as strange. But whatever people might have thought, Joseph Scriven devoted his life to helping those less fortunate than he.

The poem Joseph Scriven had written to comfort his mother was not intended to be a hymn. He hadn't meant even for anybody else to see it. It was sung for ten years as a hymn before the people of Lake Rice even knew their townsman had written it. But one day an attending neighbor found the manuscript copy in the room where Joseph Scriven lay ill. When asked if he had written the then popular hymn, the Irishman said that he and the Lord wrote it "between" them.

No one knows how the poem first got into print. Its first use as a hymn was in 1865. Nor does anyone know whether Joseph Scriven's drowning was of his own design, or if it was accidental like that of his sweetheart of so many years before. In either event, the people of Lake Rice erected a monument to the memory of the lonely Irishman who devoted his life to helping the poor.

> What a friend we have in Jesus,
>   All our sins and griefs to bear!
> What a privilege to carry
>   Ev'rything to God in prayer!
> Oh, what peace we often forfeit,
>   Oh, what needless pain we bear,
> All because we do not carry
>   Ev'rything to God in prayer!

65. "Poor Little Blind Girl"

Dr. Valentine Mott saw the little girl and her widowed mother to the door. The noted New York surgeon had made an examination of the child's eyes. But there was nothing he could do that might restore her sight.

When Fanny Jane Crosby was six weeks old, in May, 1820, she had caught a cold, and a country doctor of Putnam County, New York, had unwittingly prescribed a hot mustard poultice for her inflamed eyes. The result was total blindness for life. Soon afterward her father died. When she was five years old, sympathetic neighbors contributed money to send her to New York's famed Dr. Valentine Mott. But after an examination, Fanny Crosby heard the specialist say with a heavy heart, "Poor little blind girl." And that sympathetic expression by a great surgeon remained with Fanny Jane Crosby throughout her life.

It is no overstatement that Frances Jane Crosby Van Alstyne was one of the most remarkable women who ever lived. Resigned to Dr. Mott's verdict that her eyesight could never be restored, Fanny Crosby turned her handicap into an asset. She has even said that her blindness was a blessing, for, not being disturbed by things about her, she could more easily write her poems. At the early age of eight she wrote:

> Oh, what a happy child I am,
> Although I cannot see!
> I am resolved that in this world
> Contented I will be.

Two decades later her verse had made her famous. Among others, her "Rosalie, the Prairie Flower" and "There's Music in the Air" were set to music by composer George Frederick Root. They sold into tens of thousands of copies in sheet music.

After attending the New York Institute for the Blind, Miss Crosby was placed on the staff as an instructor. One day the superintendent found his secretary taking down verse while blind Fanny Crosby dictated. Both were warned against wasting the school's time. But the two kept up the practice, and in later years Grover Cleveland even

107

set aside affairs of state to take down verse from his ever-welcome guest at the White House.

Though devoutly religious, Fanny Crosby wrote popular verse and secular songs until she was forty-four years old. Here again the church owes a debt of gratitude to Lowell Mason's student, William Bradbury. For it was William Bradbury who in 1864 suggested to Fanny Crosby that she devote her talent to the cause of Christian worship in song. From that date Fanny Crosby never wrote another secular song. Instead, she devoted the following half century of her long life to creating gospel hymn-poems, writing more than anybody else who has ever lived—almost nine thousand!

"Poor little blind girl," Dr. Valentine Mott had said. But Fanny Crosby never regarded herself as being unfortunate in her blindness. She even said that if God should offer her normal sight, she would decline it because when she reached heaven, the first face she wanted her eyes to behold would be that of her "blessed Saviour."

Here is one of Fanny Crosby's most popular hymns. She wrote it in 1868.

> Pass me not, O gentle Saviour,
>   Hear my humble cry;
> While on others Thou art calling,
>   Do not pass me by.

> REFRAIN:
> Saviour, Saviour, Hear my humble cry;
> While on others Thou art calling, Do not pass me by.

66. A Blind Woman Takes a Hack Ride

Some writers have produced more than a hundred hymns. A few have passed the thousand mark. Charles Wesley is said to have written sixty-five hundred hymn-poems during his half century of writing. In a like number of years Fanny Crosby wrote almost six thousand sacred songs for two publishing firms. She produced fifteen hundred more for four gospel song compilers. For one firm she wrote three songs every week for years. Her total is estimated to have passed the nine thousand mark.

Critics have said that both Wesley and Fanny Crosby wrote too much. But where is the writer who has produced a masterpiece every time he took up his pen? Men of letters, it seems, are prone to appraise hymns strictly on their literary merits. But poetry is poetry, and hymns are hymns, and many a simple gospel hymn has moved multitudes where a literary masterpiece might have been sung as mere rote.

If Charles Wesley of the stately hymn or Fanny Crosby of the simpler gospel hymn wrote dross, certainly there is found in the works of each sufficient "pearls among the shells" to justify their voluminous production.

Putting aside the writing of secular ballads, Fanny Crosby threw her every fiber into her new career of producing sacred songs. In five years her fame circled the globe. She became known to evangelists and ministers on both sides of the Atlantic as "Aunt Fanny." She attended revivals and missions to study the effect of her hymns and to gather material and ideas for new ones.

On a hot night in the summer of 1869 the blind woman called a hack and rode from her home in Brooklyn to a mission in the Bowery. Word got around that the author of "Pass Me Not, O Gentle

109

Saviour" was in the audience. She was led to the speaker's platform. After delivering a talk, she stepped down to work among New York's lowest derelicts. From that experience came the inspiration for one of her most famous songs.

Riding home that night, Fanny Crosby was oblivious to the clattering traffic. As was her practice, "Aunt Fanny" formed the lines of verse in her mind and dictated them to a secretary or friend. Before she reached home the lines for "Rescue the Perishing" were formed in the mind of the blind poet. Before she retired the verses were on paper. Next morning she sent them to her friend, composer William Howard Doane, in Cincinnati.

From a strictly literary point of view, finer poetry than the following has been written. But few Christian songs have been more widely sung than this favorite which was born in the mind of a blind woman while she rode in a hack through the busy streets of New York after visiting a mission in the Bowery and telling the story of Jesus there.

> Rescue the perishing,
>   Care for the dying,
> Snatch them in pity from sin and the grave;
>   Weep o'er the erring one,
> Lift up the fallen,
>   Tell them of Jesus the mighty to save.
>
> REFRAIN:
> Rescue the perishing,
>   Care for the dying;
> Jesus is merciful,
>   Jesus will save.

67. "Bless Your Dear Soul"

All who have left a record of association with Fanny Crosby have described her as a profoundly consecrated, sincere, and lovable personality. Records have been left also of some of her personal traits. Among other things, the blind woman always carried in her hand or in her purse a small American flag. She carried also a small Bible. In making talks she always held her hand on the little Bible, for, she said, it gave her strength. By her own statement, Fanny Crosby never attempted to write a hymn without first kneeling in prayer. But perhaps the most impressive trait of this remarkable woman was that she invariably greeted friends and new acquaintances with a phrase that became the hallmark of her personality—"Bless your dear soul."

Hard put to meet her many commitments, "Aunt Fanny" had forgotten her prayer one day in 1869 when she tried to write some verses to fit a tune composer William Howard Doane had sent her. There was no inspiration. She was unable even to "create a mood." Then she remembered that she had forgotten to pray. Rising from her knees, she dictated so rapidly that her assistant had difficulty keeping up with her dictation. The hymn she wrote so rapidly that day was "Jesus, Keep Me Near the Cross."

The hymnbooks list the composer of the music to "Blessed Assurance" as "Mrs. J. F. Knapp." That's because Miss Phoebe Palmer, daughter of evangelist Walter C. Palmer, married Joseph Fairchild Knapp, founder of the Metropolitan Life Insurance Company. Encouraged by her minister-father to write music, Phoebe Palmer composed a tune in 1873 and called at the home of Fanny Crosby in Brooklyn with the request that the blind poet write some verses to go with her music.

"Bless your dear soul," Fanny Crosby greeted the young woman. "I think your music is beautiful. Play it for me on the organ."

As Phoebe Palmer played her composition, she turned to see "Aunt Fanny" kneeling in prayer. She played it a second time. She had just begun to play it a third time when her hostess rose and began dictating, "Blessed assurance, Jesus is mine! Oh, what a foretaste of glory divine! Heir of salvation, purchase of God, Born of His spirit, wash'd in His blood."

One day in 1874 Fanny Crosby prayed for more material things. She was short of money and needed five dollars. There was no time to draw on her publishers. So she simply prayed for the money. Rising from her knees, she was walking the room trying to "get into the mood" for another hymn when the doorbell rang. She greeted the strange admirer with, "Bless your dear soul," and the two chatted briefly. According to Fanny Crosby's statement, in the parting handshake the strange caller left something in her hand. It was five dollars. From that experience the blind poet wrote:

> All the way my Saviour leads me;
> What have I to ask beside?
> Can I doubt His tender mercy,
> Who thro' life has been my guide?
> Heav'nly peace, divinest comfort,
> Here by faith in Him to dwell!
> For I know whate'er befall me,
> Jesus doeth all things well.

68. A Hat-maker Writes a Tune

The music for "Pass Me Not, O Gentle Saviour," "Near the Cross," "Saviour, More than Life to Me," "Rescue the Perishing," "I Am Thine, O Lord," and many, many more inspiring gospel hymns is from the pen of William Howard Doane. For almost a century hymnals of most Protestant denominations have included a liberal selection of Doane's compositions. It has been said that "there is scarcely a place on earth where civilization has pushed its way that the influence of Dr. Doane has not been felt."

But Dr. William Howard Doane was a businessman. The writing of music with him was an avocation. And it is interesting to note that in the writing of hymns such is the rule rather than the exception.

Silas Jones Vail was a manufacturer of hats. As a young man Vail left his home in Brooklyn, where he was born in 1818, and went to Danbury, Connecticut. There he learned the trade of hatmaking. He

then returned to New York City, where he established his own hat manufacturing business.

Like machinery manufacturer William Howard Doane, hat manufacturer Silas Jones Vail's principal love and avocation was the composition of music. Like Doane, Vail, too, ventured into the publication of songbooks. In 1863, with pious publisher Horace Waters, he bought ten songs from mild-mannered Stephen Foster, added a sizeable collection of others, and published a book called *The Anthenaeum Collection.* And while the nation was singing Foster's songs about an old home in Kentucky and a fictional cabin on Florida's snake-infested Sewanee River, churchgoers from the Atlantic to the Pacific were singing the music Silas Jones Vail wrote for "Scatter Seeds of Kindness," "Nothing but Leaves," and "Gates Ajar."

In 1874 Vail turned from his business enterprises to compile and edit with composer W. F. Sherwin a songbook called *Songs of Grace and Glory.* During this work he wrote an original tune, but there were no words for the music. And as Fanny Crosby was the most celebrated writer of gospel hymn-poems, Vail's thoughts turned to the blind poet in nearby Brooklyn.

While blind Fanny Crosby listened, Silas Vail played his tune on the parlor organ. Vail had not even completed playing the refrain when the poet stopped him. "Bless your dear soul," the sightless little woman said, "Your music speaks its own words. It says, 'Close to Thee . . . close to Thee.'" Then, after her prayer, she dictated while her composer-guest took down these words.

> Thou, my everlasting portion,
>   More than friend or life to me;
> All along my pilgrim journey,
>   Saviour, let me walk with Thee.

> REFRAIN:
> Close to Thee, close to Thee,
>   Close to Thee, close to Thee;

All along my pilgrim journey,
Saviour, let me walk with Thee.

69. Fanny Crosby Writes Her Last

The lady of the house at Bridgeport, Connecticut, rapped gently at the door of the room where the blind woman made her home. Aunt Fanny Crosby had not come out of the room all morning, and it was nearly time for the parade. The lady rapped again. When still there was no answer, she opened the door. Fanny Crosby lay just as she had retired the night before. Sometime during the night her soul had slipped away.

Near the bed, on a writing table, was her little American flag. On the table, too, was a letter of consolation to parents of a little neighbor girl who had died the day before. Taken partly from one of her hymns, it was her last poem. It read:

> You will reach the river brink
> Some sweet day, by and by,
> You will find your broken link
> Some sweet day, by and by.
>
> O the loved ones waiting there
> By the tree of life so fair,
> 'Til you come, their joy to share,
> Some sweet day, by and by.

So closed, on February 12, 1915, the career of Frances Jane Crosby Van Alstyne, the most prolific writer of Christian songs who ever lived. She had known happiness. And she had known sorrow. Her only child had died in infancy. Her blind musician-husband, with whom she had happily shared a quarter of a century, had long since found "rest beyond the river."

Fanny Crosby had known more United States presidents than anybody who had ever lived. Abraham Lincoln was her favorite. That's why she had put the flag on the table. She had meant to wave it in the parade commemorating Lincoln's birthday.

Fanny Crosby had lost her sight at the age of six weeks. She never remembered having seen the light of day. But strangely she cheerfully insisted that her blindness was a blessing. Undisturbed by distractions about her, she said, she could write more easily. She said too that by being blind on earth, when her sight was restored in heaven, the first sight her eyes would behold would be that of her "blessed Saviour."

Friends put the little flag in Aunt Fanny's hand. It was buried with her. As someone said, the angels might want her to lead a parade in heaven. At the funeral services her own hymns were sung. One was "Safe in the Arms of Jesus." Another was this one which she wrote early in her career, in 1869, for a tune her friend William Howard Doane had sent her.

> Jesus, keep me near the cross,
>   There a precious fountain,
> Free to all, a healing stream,
>   Flows from Calv'ry's mountain.

> REFRAIN:
> In the cross, in the cross
>   Be my glory ever,
> Till my raptur'd soul shall find
>   Rest beyond the river.

70. A General Reads a Poem

The General walked onto the stage. He held some leaves of paper in his hand. When the applause subsided, he began reading two long poems.

England's Major General Russell was the man of the hour. Ireland's revolutionary Fenians had chosen the last months of America's War Between the States to strike at British rule, and blood had flowed on the homeland and in southern Canada. But Russell and his troops had put down the uprising, and the General, an international hero, was selected to represent England at the YMCA's International convention at Montreal in 1867.

The poem General Russell read had been written a year earlier by the bed-ridden daughter of a London banker. Her name was Catherine Arabelle Hankey. Some hymnals list her as "Katherine" or "Kate" Hankey.

Doctors told Kate Hankey she would die if she didn't take to her bed and remain there at least a year. She was forbidden to do missionary work or teach her Bible class of working girls. So Kate Hankey took to her bed, but she carried with her a stack of writing paper. That was in January, 1866, when Miss Hankey was thirty years old.

To keep her mind off her illness, the delicate young woman wrote a fifty-stanza poem. She called it "The Story Wanted." Then she wrote a sequel. It too was fifty stanzas long. She called it "The Story Told."

After ten months, Kate Hankey grew tired of writing in bed. She got up and went to South Africa to visit an invalid brother. She rode in and out of the jungles in an ox cart. Then she went back to London and resumed her missionary work and Bible school teaching. But, as she had been warned, she died—half a century later.

When General Russell got to the lines "Tell me the story simply,

116

as to a little child . . . ," his eyes blurred. Tears streamed down his bronzed face. His voice broke, but he held the convention spellbound through the one hundred stanzas.

After General Russell finished reading, Cincinnati's YMCA delegate William Howard Doane copied some of the verses. That afternoon, while riding in a stagecoach to his resort hotel in the White Mountains, he composed a tune. Selecting four stanzas from Miss Hankey's first poem, "The Story Wanted," he wedded the lines to his music. (The hymn "I Love to Tell the Story" is taken from the second poem, "The Story Told.") That evening in the hotel parlor Doane called a group of friends together, and they sang this hymn for the first time.

> Tell me the old, old story
>   Of unseen things above,
> Of Jesus and His glory,
>   Of Jesus and His love:
> Tell me the story simply,
>   As to a little child,
> For I am weak and weary,
>   And helpless and defiled.

> REFRAIN:
> Tell me the old, old story,
>   Tell me the old, old story,
> Tell me the old, old story
>   Of Jesus and His love.

71. "I've Been Looking for You for Eight Years"

"I'm afraid that boy will never amount to anything," lamented bank president Sankey of his son Ira David. "All he does is run about the country with a hymnbook under his arm."

Ira David Sankey grew up in New Castle, Pennsylvania. As a young man he was choir director and Sunday school superintendent at the Methodist church there. As an employee of his father's bank he spent more time "running about the country" to singing conventions than he spent at his banking job. At the age of thirty, in 1870, he was an employee of the Internal Revenue Department, the father of two children, and in that year a delegate to the YMCA convention at Indianapolis, Indiana.

Slipping in late during a lengthy prayer at one of the convention meetings, delegate Sankey chanced to sit next to a man who knew of his singing ability. That chance event was to change the course of Sankey's life and the history of evangelism in America and England.

"When that fellow gets through praying," Sankey's neighbor whispered, "I wish you would start a song. The singing here has been terrible."

The song Ira Sankey led the delegates in singing was William Cowper's age-old favorite, "There Is a Fountain Filled with Blood." Present at the convention was a delegate from Chicago. He was evangelist Dwight L. Moody. Seeking out Sankey after the adjournment, Moody said to the big song leader with the lamb-chop sideburns, "I've been looking for you for eight years."

The following year, with only "a songbook, a Bible, and their reputations," Moody and Sankey launched the most fabulous series of revival campaigns in history.

During a campaign in Ireland in 1874, Sankey read a poem on a small printed leaflet. The verses had been written by an Irish preacher named Samuel O'Malley Cluff (sometimes spelled Clough). Little is known about Mr. Cluff except that he was once a clergyman in the Established Church, broke with that denomination to join the Plymouth Brethren, and later left the Brethren to join yet another denomination.

It is probable that the shifting Cluff's poem would have been forgotten but for the ability of a man who, as a youth, had "run about the hills of Pennsylvania with a hymnbook under his arm." For

when Ira David Sankey read Mr. Cluff's poem, he saw in it material
for an appealing gospel hymn. He set the stanzas to music and sang
them all over Ireland, Scotland, England, and America. The Christian world has been singing the hymn ever since.

> I have a Saviour, He's pleading in glory,
>   A dear loving Saviour, tho' earth-friends be few;
> And now He is watching in tenderness o'er me,
>   And, oh, that my Saviour were your Saviour, too.

> REFRAIN:
> For you I am praying,
>   For you I am praying;
> For you I am praying,
>   I'm praying for you.

72. A Preacher and a Singer Take a Train Ride

Two tired men hurried through the railroad station
at Glasgow, Scotland. One was short and stout, with iron-grey hair.
The other was tall and massive with sideburns that blended into a
heavy mustache. The short man was Dwight Lyman Moody, the
one-time shoe clerk who started preaching from a packing box and
became the best-known evangelist of the nineteenth century. The
tall man was Ira David Sankey, the one-time bank clerk who sang
solos to his own accompaniment and became the best-known revival
song leader in history.

Sankey paused, bought a newspaper, and stuffed it into his pocket. The two had just closed an extended revival campaign in Glasgow and were on their way to Edinburgh for a belated engagement. The train had hardly pulled out of the station when Moody waded into a bundle of unopened letters from his headquarters in Chicago. It was 1874. His church had been destroyed three years earlier in the great fire, and he was anxious to know about progress on his new tabernacle.

Sankey scanned his newspaper, but there was nothing of particular interest. He tossed the paper aside. The train rocked on through the night. The indefatigable Moody read his letters, made notes. Sankey scanned his paper again. He was about to cast it aside a second time when he noticed a poem on a corner of one of the pages. It had been written by an orphaned Scottish girl named Elizabeth Clephane. It had first been published in a children's magazine, and the young poetess had died five years before the Glasgow newspaper reprinted the verses to fill out the page. Ira Sankey read the lines over and over. He tore the poem out, put in into his pocket, and forgot it.

In Edinburgh, Moody's first sermon was on the subject of "The Good Shepherd." The time came for Sankey's solo, but the singer had not been foretold of the subject and had no appropriate selection. Under the circumstances he had not even anticipated doing a solo. Then he thought of the poem. Strangely enough, the words suited the subject exactly. But there was no music for the verses.

Ira Sankey has said that he put the newspaper clipping on the music rack and breathed a prayer. His hands dropped to the keys. He struck a melody and started singing. He has said too that those few moments were the "most intense" of his life. And this is, perhaps, the only case in the history of hymn writing where a tune was composed, note for note, just as it stands today, while the composer sang it for the first time.

His solo over, Sankey bowed his head. The congregation was spellbound. Moody came from the pulpit, leaned over the organ and asked Sankey, "Where on earth did you get that hymn?"

Sankey merely pointed to the newspaper clipping.

> There were ninety and nine that safely lay
> In the shelter of the fold,

But one was out on the hills away,
Far off from the gates of gold.
Away on the mountain wild and bare,
Away from the tender Shepherd's care.

73. An Ailing Minister Turns to Hymn Writing

It was a Sunday in March, 1877. The preaching service was over at Philadelphia's Arch Street Methodist Church. A group of men lingered outside. One of them was a retired minister who had been out of the pulpit for three years. Twice before he had retired due to ill health. But his health had failed again when he was sixty-one, and he reckoned his active days to be over. Now, at sixty-four, he was hardly able to get about.

Rev. John Hart Stockton was reared a Presbyterian in New Hope, Pennsylvania, where he was born in 1813. At the age of nineteen he attended a Methodist camp meeting and changed to that denomination. He had wanted to be a minister, but not until he was forty-four years old did he venture to assume the responsibilities of a full-time charge. Even then he was in and out of active service as his health would permit.

Mr. Stockton loved music and poetry. When he didn't feel up to preaching, he spent his time writing hymns. By the time he decided to retire for the final time, he had written so many hymns that he published them in two volumes. One he called *Salvation Melodies;* the other was entitled *Precious Songs.*

On his travels evangelistic singer Ira David Sankey invariably kept

121

at hand what he called his "musical scrapbook." Into the collection went an assortment of verse and music for meditation and study as Sankey's full schedule would permit.

Crossing the Atlantic in June, 1873, Ira Sankey found time for work on material in his scrapbook. He came across a hymn by Mr. Stockton that began, "Come, every soul by sin oppressed, there's mercy with the Lord . . ." Sankey was impressed with the music and the verses, but he wasn't much pleased with the chorus that began, "Come to Jesus, come to Jesus, come to Jesus now . . ." So he changed the lines to read, "Only trust Him, only trust Him, Only trust Him now. . . ." And he sang it that way at the great revivals in England where he lead the singing for evangelist Dwight L. Moody. The song became so popular that Sankey wrote Mr. Stockton that he thanked God for such "sweet music, as well as words."

John Hart Stockton wrote "sweet music" also for the words of other writers. The world is still singing, among many others, his music to Rev. Elisha Hoffman's camp meeting favorite, "Down at the cross where my Saviour died . . ." And in the winter of 1875, when Moody and Sankey came to Philadelphia, John Hart Stockton helped Ira Sankey with the singing.

Perhaps the men who gathered to talk outside Philadelphia's Arch Street Church that Sunday in March, 1877, noticed that their retired minister friend wasn't feeling so well, or perhaps they didn't. But whatever the subject, the conversation was cut short. For as the men talked, John Hart Stockton collapsed and died. He wasn't quite sixty-five, but what matters a few years in the life of a man who left to the world so great a heritage of "sweet music, as well as words"?

> Come, ev'ry soul by sin oppressed,
>   There's mercy with the Lord,
> And He will surely give you rest
>   By trusting in His word.
>
> REFRAIN:
> Only trust Him, only trust Him,
>   Only trust Him now;
> He will save you, He will save you,
>   He will save you now.

74. "The Greatest American Hymn Writer"

The works of John Greenleaf Whittier stand in the forefront of American literature. Yet the renowned poet did not finish high school. Critics have singled out Whittier as the greatest American hymn writer. And the most scholarly hymnals include his works. However, Whittier said of himself, "I am really not a hymn writer for the good reason that I know nothing of music." And he added, "A good hymn is the best use to which poetry can be devoted, but I do not claim that I have succeeded in composing one."

Whittier knew little of church music. Being a Quaker, he never sang in church. The few hymns that he wrote as such are said to be of poor quality, and most of them have been forgotten. Yet no less than seventy-five of the world's finest hymns have come from his pen —more than from any other of America's great poets. The explanation is simply that from Whittier's poems selections of verse have been set to music. Thus through no intention of his own, John Greenleaf Whittier has become America's greatest hymn writer.

But Whittier could not have written poetry adaptable as hymns had he not possessed a simple and sincere faith in God. Whittier did not "climb the heavenly steeps" nor "search the lowest deeps" in his quest of God. God was with Whittier wherever Whittier was—as a laborer on his father's farm in Massachusetts, as a cobbler working his way through two six-month terms at Haverhill Academy, as an inspired youth listening to a wandering Scotsman sing the songs of Robert Burns, as a state legislator, as a newspaper editor, and as the author of the immortal "Snowbound," "Ichabod," and "At Sundown." And God was with John Greenleaf Whittier in 1892 when on his deathbed he whispered, "Love . . . love to all the world."

Pomp and rituals had no place in Whittier's worship. To Whittier, the degree of man's belief in God was reflected in the way he made use of the life God had given him. "O brother man! fold to thy heart thy brother," he once wrote. "To worship rightly is to love each other, Each smile a hymn, each kindly deed a prayer." That was John Greenleaf Whittier's theology.

In 1872, at the age of sixty-five, the poet wrote a seventeen-stanza poem, "The Brewing of Soma." In the poem he painted a picture of ancient priests brewing an intoxicating potion to the mythical Hindu goddess and of the boisterous rituals that followed the drinking. Applying his theme to modern times, the poet wrote, "We brew in many a Christian clime, the heathen Soma still." It was from this poem, written to emphasize what was to Whittier the folly of ceremony in worship, that these lines have been selected to form what has been called the finest hymn of true worship in literature.

> Dear Lord and Father of mankind,
>   Forgive our foolish ways;
> Reclothe us in our rightful mind;
>   In purer lives Thy service find,
> In deeper rev'rence, praise.

75. A Housewife Writes a Hymn

It has been said that every hymn has its story. The problem lies in finding the story.

Most hymns of lasting worth are the result of events or experiences that particularly moved the authors to write them. But there are exceptions. The exception rather than the rule shows in the writing of "I Need Thee Every Hour."

Anne Sherwood Hawks was in the best of health. She had not a care in the world. No comfort was lacking in her Brooklyn home. She was in the prime of life. She was the idol of a devoted husband and family.

On a clear day in June, 1872, Anne Sherwood Hawks was so happy

that her thoughts turned to a feeling of gratitude to God for her many blessings. "I remember well the morning," she wrote in recalling that day. She said she felt a sense of "nearness to the Master . . . and these words 'I need Thee every hour' were ushered into my mind."

So it was during "hours of sweet security and peace" that Mrs. Hawks put her housework aside and "on the wings of love and joy" wrote her famous hymn-poem.

The writing of poetry was not new with Anne Sherwood Hawks. Ever since she was a teen-age girl in Hoosick, New York, where she was born in 1835, she had written verse. Moving to Brooklyn in 1857, she united with the Hanson Place Baptist Church and was further encouraged in her writing by her pastor, Rev. Robert Lowry.

Mrs. Hawks gave her poem, "I Need Thee Every Hour," to Dr. Lowry. Lowry, author-composer of many a notable hymn—including "Shall We Gather at the River?"—wrote a chorus and set the verses to music. The new hymn was first sung in public in November of that year at the National Baptist Sunday School Convention in Cincinnati. Its popularity was spontaneous. Dr. Lowry published it in his songbook, *Royal Diadem*. Ira Sankey sang it at the great revivals led by Dwight L. Moody in England and America. It echoed through the auditoriums of Chicago's World's Colombian Exposition.

Regarding her hymn's popularity, Mrs. Hawks said, "I do not understand why it so touched the great throbbing heart of humanity." But in 1888, sixteen years later, the housewife who had once known only "hours of sweet security and peace" understood. She has said that the death of her devoted husband cast a "shadow of a great loss" over her life. And for the thirty years that followed, until she herself died in 1918, Anne Sherwood Hawks turned to her own hymn for comfort.

And so while the poet did not come to appreciate fully the meaning of her poem until long after she had written it, there is, after all, a story in the writing of this hymn.

I need Thee ev'ry hour,
    Most gracious Lord;
No tender voice like Thine
    Can peace afford.

REFRAIN:
I need Thee, O I need Thee;
    Ev'ry hour I need Thee!
O bless me now, my Saviour,
    I come to Thee.

76. An Artist Goes to Camp Meeting

Three miles wide, twenty miles long, and fourteen hundred feet above sea level, Lake Chautauqua in southwestern New York State is one of the most picturesque spots in the world. That is one reason Methodists have held camp meetings there for more than a century.

In the summer of 1873, while churchmen and laymen gathered at Lake Chautauqua, an unassuming artist bent over her drawing board in New York City to turn out illustrations for magazines and books for children. The illustrator modestly signed her work "M. A. L." Her name was Mary Artemisia Lathbury.

Weary of being confined to her studio and plagued by poor eyesight, the thirty-two-year-old artist decided to close shop and take a rest. She had heard her Methodist minister-father and her two Methodist minister-brothers speak of picturesque Lake Chautauqua and the camp meetings held there each summer. So Mary Lathbury turned westward to Lake Chautauqua.

At the camp meeting grounds Miss Lathbury met Tuscaloosa, Alabama's ever-busy Bishop John H. Vincent. In addition to editing *The Sunday School Quarterly* and *The Sunday School Teacher* and inaugurating the Sunday school lesson system, Vincent was busy also

as executive secretary of the Methodist Sunday School Union. So busy was Dr. Vincent that Miss Lathbury volunteered to help with details of his work.

During the following summer, with Lewis Miller, Vincent inaugurated an educational system that was soon to become famous as the "Chautauqua Movement." By 1877 "Chautauqua" had spread across the nation. Four hundred thousand people were on the rolls. During the summers fifty thousand people gathered at the lake to attend lectures, study, listen to camp meeting sermons, and sing in the mammoth choir directed by Baptist music director William Fiske Sherwin of Boston.

Inspired by Sherwin's great choir, Dr. Vincent remarked to Miss Lathbury that it would be fitting if the Chautauqua Movement had a vesper hymn especially its own. That afternoon Mary Lathbury slipped away to a hillside overlooking the lake. By the time the sun had gone down, she had written a poem. She wrote over it "Day Is Dying in the West" and gave it to music director Sherwin. Sherwin set it to music, and the hymn has been called "one of the finest and most distinctive hymns of modern times."

Artist Mary Lathbury became known as "the lyrist of Chautauqua." All across America people sang "Day Is Dying in the West." And all across America people joined Chautauqua literary and scientific circles.

In 1880 Bishop Vincent remarked to Miss Lathbury that it would be fitting if Chautauqua circles had a study song for members to sing at their gatherings. So Mary Lathbury went back to the hillside overlooking the lake. This time she carried with her a Bible. Turning to the story of Christ feeding the multitude at the Sea of Galilee, she likened the scene to that of the milling throngs along the banks of Lake Chautauqua. And she wrote this famous hymn which choir director Sherwin also set to music.

> Break Thou the bread of life, Dear Lord, to me,
> As Thou didst break the loaves beside the sea;

Beyond the sacred page I seek Thee, Lord;
My spirit pants for Thee, O living Word.

77. A Despairing Crusader Turns to God

"Tainted money!" That's what Rev. Washington Gladden called a check for one hundred thousand dollars. It was not that the venerable minister objected to so sizeable a donation for furthering the cause of Christianity in foreign lands; what raised his blood pressure was the thought of where his Board of Foreign Missions got the donation. For the board had solicited, of all people, the very man whose "monopolistic practices" had been Gladden's principal target for years—John D. Rockefeller, Sr.

For three decades, beginning immediately before the turn of the century, the name of Congregational minister Washington Gladden was on the lips of practically every corporation board member in America.

After eleven years in pulpits of the East, the native Pennsylvanian resigned the ministry to carry on his fight for social reform in the broader media of the press. But after four years on the editorial staff of the New York *Independent,* during which time the editorialist-clergyman helped put Tammany boss Tweed behind bars for fifteen years, the crusader returned to the pulpit to again take up the torch for his cause. Nor did he put aside his crusading pen. His forceful articles were carried in periodicals from coast to coast for almost half a century.

It was in 1882 that Dr. Gladden began an uninterrupted thirty-four-year period in the pulpit of the Columbus, Ohio, First Congre-

gational Church. It was an era of budding—and blooming—monopolies. During the early 1900's the courageous crusader held high the torch for Teddy Roosevelt's fight against depredations of combined capital. On Sunday mornings he preached the gospel from an assorted selection of texts. But on Sunday evenings he preached the gospel from a single text. Year in and year out, Gladden's Sunday evening subject was "applied Christianity between employer and employee."

Obviously, Dr. Gladden made enemies among the rich. Because of his liberalism, some of his fellow clergymen turned their backs on him. After his attacks on Rockefeller in his articles "Standard Oil and Foreign Missions" and "Tainted Money," the crusading minister was all but turned out of his denomination. At times he felt that he had not a friend in the world.

It was during one of these hours of discouragement and despair in 1879, after his congregation at Springfield, Massachusetts, had grown hostile toward him, that Dr. Gladden sat alone in his church and wrote this hymn.

O Master, let me walk with Thee
In lowly paths of service free;
Tell me Thy secret, help me bear
The strain of toil, the fret of care.

78. The Most Rapidly Written of All Hymns

Timothy Dwight, early president of Yale University and author of "I Love Thy Kingdom, Lord," was blinded by smallpox and excessive use of his eyes. Henry Smart, composer of "Lead on, O King Eternal" and many another hymn tune, spent the last fifteen years of his life in total blindness. Singer-composer Ira D. Sankey lost his eyesight in the sunset of life. Prolific writer Fanny Crosby was blinded in infancy. These are but a few of a long list.

Perhaps to compensate for the loss of his sight nature endowed Scottish minister George Matheson with what is sometimes referred to as a photographic mind. For Matheson could memorize page after page of written matter and recite it word for word after hearing it read two times. It was his practice to dictate sermons to his sister, have her read them back twice, and then deliver them word for word in the pulpit.

Such was Dr. Matheson's invariable procedure for twelve years at Scotland's seaport town of Inellan, where he had taken his first church in 1868. But one Sunday in 1880 the thirty-eight-year-old blind minister's remarkable mind failed him. As was his practice, he turned pages of the Bible to give the effect of reading. But he could not remember a word of his prepared sermon. Calmly, he announced a different subject and preached his first extemporaneous sermon. After thus discovering his native talent for oratory, Matheson became one of the greatest preachers of the last century. At forty-four he was called to Edinburgh's St. Bernard's Church with its two thousand members, and he was summoned to preach before Queen Victoria at Balmoral Castle.

In June, 1882, relatives went to Glasgow for the wedding of Dr. Matheson's sister. In the loneliness of his study, "something happened," he wrote, "which caused me the most severe mental suffering." He never said what the suffering was. Some believe that his sister's marriage brought back memories of his college days when, it is said, his fiancé declined to marry him because of his failing eyes.

The upshot of Matheson's "severe mental suffering" was that he wrote a hymn, which he later said "was the quickest bit of work I ever did in my life." He said that "some inward voice" seemed to dictate the lines and that he was "quite sure the whole work was completed in five minutes." And this is all the more remarkable when one considers that Dr. Matheson could not see the paper on which he was writing.

Singularly, the music for this remarkably beautiful hymn was composed with similar rapidity. Composer A. L. Peace has stated, "The ink of the first note was hardly dry when I had composed the tune."

Here are lines of verse which have been called "poetry of the highest order." Yet, according to the author, all four stanzas were completed in five minutes. Granting that to be true, this is quite likely the most rapidly written of all hymns.

> O Love that wilt not let me go,
> I rest my weary soul in thee;
> I give thee back the life I owe,
> That in thine ocean depths its flow
> May richer, fuller be.

79. A Young Man Testifies

To whatever else the state of Pennsylvania might lay claim can be added a fair share of the nation's composers of music, both religious and secular. Among those in the former group identified with the Keystone State are James McGranahan, composer of "Showers of Blessing"; Ira David Sankey, "The Ninety and Nine"; Philip Bliss, "Wonderful Words of Life"; William Kirkpatrick, "Jesus Saves"; and Daniel B. Towner of the town of Rome, from whence came also Philip Bliss.

Added to whatever there is about Pennsylvania that might be conducive to the development of musical talent, Daniel B. Towner had also the advantage of being reared in a family of musicians and singers. His father, J. G. Towner, taught young Daniel to sing and to read notes before the boy was old enough to read the letters of the alphabet.

After writing music, teaching, singing, and directing choirs in New

York, Cincinnati, and numerous other cities, Daniel Towner joined evangelist Dwight L. Moody's corps of song directors in 1885. One evening, in response to Moody's invitation for personal testimony during a revival at Brockton, Massachusetts, a young man rose and said, "I am not sure . . . but I am going to trust and obey." From that phrase was born a gospel hymn by which Daniel Towner has been remembered ever since.

Towner wrote the phrase down on paper. He sent the line and a letter explaining the circumstances to his Presbyterian minister-friend J. H. Sammis in Indiana. Rev. Sammis was a native New Yorker turned midwesterner. He was later an executive of the Los Angeles Bible Institute and author of a hundred hymn-poems. Receiving Towner's letter with the young penitent's testimonial phrase, "I am going to trust and obey," Sammis wrote some verses around the theme and sent them back to song leader Towner. Towner set the poem to music.

Like many another of his fellow Pennsylvanians, Daniel B. Towner spent his entire life singing and furthering the cause of worship in song. He literally began singing at his father's knee. He was thirty-five years old when he joined the Moody camp. For Moody and other evangelists he sang all over America and much of Europe. He was still singing in his seventieth year when, on October 3, 1919, he was stricken at a revival in Missouri and died. And the world is still singing his music to many a gospel hymn, especially the one that was inspired by a young penitent who said of his salvation that he was not sure but that he would "trust and obey."

When we walk with the Lord
    In the light of His Word
What a glory He sheds on our way!
    While we do His good will,
He abides with us still,
    And with all who will trust and obey.

REFRAIN:
Trust and obey,
    For there's no other way
To be happy in Jesus,
    But to trust and obey.

132

80. A Minister Ponders the Hulk of a Ship

Waves lapped against the broken old hulk. The tide came in and went out. The summer sun shone, and the snows of winter came. But the old ship never moved. Nobody knew where the storm-wrecked vessel came from. Nobody knew when it had been washed upon the rock-bound coast of Massachusetts. It was just there, and that's all anybody knew.

Ships and the sea fascinated young Rev. Edward Smith Ufford. On his journeys to Boston from the nearby town of Westwood, where he lived and where he preached at the Baptist church, Mr. Ufford usually took the long way around so he could stop and look at the old ship. In his fancy—or in his "mind's eye," as he put it—the young minister could see the proud vessel as she once had sailed the seas in all her glory. He pictured the storm that broke her apart. He saw men washed overboard to drown. He could hear their calls for help, and finally, he envisioned the cruel waves as they dashed her helplessly ashore—to rot and rust and be forgotten. There, thought the thirty-four-year-old minister, was a lesson for mankind.

One Sunday afternoon in the autumn of 1886 Mr. Ufford hauled his little organ to the scene and began preaching. During his "sidewalk" sermon he pointed to the ship. After his message the subject lingered in his mind. He pondered writing a hymn around the theme of saving men who had been wrecked on the sea of life. But at the moment he could not fit the lines together.

Shortly afterward Mr. Ufford visited a lifesaving station at Nantasket Beach. An attendant showed the minister a silken lifeline and explained its usage. Coiling the line, the attendant swung his arms with a gesture and said, "This is how we throw out the lifeline."

That phrase during the demonstration was all Ufford needed. "Returning home," he said, "I wrote the four stanzas of the hymn in fifteen minutes." He then composed the melody "with but little effort."

A few weeks later composer George C. Stebbins was leading music at a revival at Lawrence, Massachusetts, when his attention was directed to a copy of Mr. Ufford's song. Stebbins, composer of hundreds of gospel hymns, bought the song, rearranged the harmony, and had it published in *Gospel Hymns*. From there it spread around the world.

The old hulk is gone. Nobody remembers when it disappeared. Around Boston old-timers still talk of a great tornado that struck the New England seaboard in 1888. Maybe the old hulk was ripped to pieces then. Or perhaps when the tide was right she went back to sea. Nobody knows. But while she lay helpless on the rocks, she inspired the writing of this hymn that has outlived many a gallant ship since her time.

> Throw out the lifeline across the dark wave,
>   There is a brother whom someone should save;
> Somebody's brother! Oh, who then, will dare
>   To throw out the lifeline, his peril to share?

> REFRAIN:
> Throw out the lifeline! Throw out the lifeline!
>   Someone is drifting away;
> Throw out the lifeline! Throw out the lifeline!
>   Someone is sinking today.

81. A Singing Master Answers His Mail

Time was in America when only those who could afford private instruction were taught to sing by note. Prior to 1830 and the advent of the "Lowell Mason era" there were few hymn-

books. Churchgoers depended on song leaders to read a hymn line by line and set the tune.

Among his many other contributions to furthering Christian worship in song, Mason trained teachers and sent them into rural communities where they organized "singing classes" and taught the masses to sing. These teachers in turn taught others to teach. And by 1900 the tune-setter and hymn-reader had practically vanished. Today in America the influence of Lowell Mason is legion. Tens of thousands of people, especially in the South, recall with fond memory the experience of attending "singing classes" under the direction of an itinerant singing master. Among the most widely known and influential of the twentieth century masters was Virginia's composer-publisher-teacher A. J. Showalter.

One night in 1887 Professor Showalter dismissed his class at Hartselle, Alabama. He collected his songbooks, closed the church where his classes were held, and drove to the rooming house where he had "put up" for his brief stay in the north Alabama town.

In his room the professor opened letters from two former pupils in South Carolina. Each of the letters contained identical news. Each of the pupils had recently lost his wife, both on the same day. In an effort to console his two young friends, A. J. Showalter turned to the Bible. He began writing: "The eternal God is thy refuge, and underneath are the everlasting arms."

A. J. Showalter wrote a third letter that night in 1887. For in that line of Scripture lay the theme for a Christian song—a song of consolation for others like his two former pupils who might be burdened with sorrow. He wrote a chorus and sent it with a letter to hymn-writer Elisha Hoffman in Pennsylvania. Mr. Hoffman, author of "I Must Tell Jesus," "Glory to His Name," and two thousand other hymn-poems, wrote three stanzas and sent them back to Professor Showalter in Alabama. The singing master set the verses and his chorus to music. Thus was born a gospel hymn that is found in many a stately hymnal.

135

At the age of seventy, in 1927, A. J. Showalter led his last earthly singing at Chattanooga, Tennessee. He left behind hundreds of gospel song compositions. He left also thousands of pupils who remember him to this day. For like Lowell Mason, the followers of A. J. Showalter are legion. But long after the name of A. J. Showalter has been forgotten, the world will be singing a Christian song, the writing of which was inspired when this itinerant singing master sought to console two bereaved young men.

> What a fellowship, what a joy divine,
>   Leaning on the everlasting arms;
> What a blessedness, what a peace is mine,
>   Leaning on the everlasting arms.

> REFRAIN:
> Leaning, leaning,
>   Safe and secure from all alarms;
> Leaning, leaning,
>   Leaning on the everlasting arms.

82. An Author Who Wanted No Recognition

Rev. Edward Hopper settled back in the easy chair of his study. He had a weak heart and at seventy-two was living on borrowed time. But on that day in April, 1888, he felt up to writing; so he took pencil and paper and started outlining the words of another hymn. Nobody knows how many hymn-poems the modest Presbyterian minister wrote. He rarely signed them, and when he did affix a name, it was usually fictitious.

During the week Mr. Hopper worked among the sailors. On Sundays he preached to them at New York Harbor's "Church of the Sea and Land." But when he cast his bread upon the waters through his hymn writing, he always chose to remain anonymous.

Edward Hopper was a man of the city. He was born and educated in New York. After pastorates at Greenville, New York, and at Sag Harbor on Long Island, he was elected to the church at the harbor where the congregation was made up mostly of sailors.

Like Methodist Charles Wesley, who wrote hymns suited to his various congregations, Edward Hopper wrote for the men who go down to the sea in ships. Among his "sailor" hymns are "They Pray the Best Who Pray and Watch" and "Wrecked and Struggling in Mid-ocean."

In 1871 one of Mr. Hopper's hymn-poems was published in the *Sailors' Magazine*. Philadelphia's ailing composer, John Edgar Gould, set it to music the night before he sailed for Africa, where he hoped to mend his failing health. When it was later learned that Gould had died in Algiers, the sailors mourned the death of the man who had set "Jesus, Saviour, Pilot Me" to music. But none of Edward Hopper's congregation suspected that their own pastor had written the words.

On April 23, 1888, friends found Edward Hopper seated in his easy chair. A pencil was in his hand. A sheet of paper had settled on the floor. On the paper was the beginning of a hymn-poem. The title was "Heaven," but there was no name of the author under the title. Even had the hymn been finished, it is doubtful that anybody would have known who had written it. For years the sailors at New York Harbor's "Church of the Sea and Land" had sung "Jesus, Saviour, Pilot Me" while Mr. Hopper sat in the pulpit, and nobody in the congregation knew who wrote the hymn.

But among papers found in Edward Hopper's study were original manuscripts of many a hymn-poem. And among them was "Jesus, Saviour, Pilot Me."

> Jesus, Saviour, pilot me
> Over life's tempestuous sea;
> Unknown waves before me roll,
> Hiding rock and treach'rous shoal;

Chart and compass came from Thee:
Jesus, Saviour, pilot me.

83. A Hymn That Was Written by Two Young Men

Henry Smart's father was a violinist and piano-maker. He knew practically every musician in London, which might account for his enrolling his musically inclined son in law school. But young Henry Smart wanted no part of the legal profession. Shortly after quitting law school he was offered a commission in the Indian army, but he declined. He wanted only to be a musician.

Except for limited training by a sympathetic London violinist, Henry Smart educated himself in music. He worked and studied so intently that by the time he was twenty-three years old, he had done two things that were to affect the rest of his life—he had composed a tune which he called "Lancashire" for the celebration of the three hundredth anniversary of the Reformation, and he had impaired his eyesight by overwork.

In later years Henry Smart became famous as an organist. He produced 250 secular compositions. He edited hymnals and contributed considerably of his talents to the church. But it was the tune "Lancashire" that made his reputation. It was his hallmark. The lively composition was picked up by vocalists from Greenland's icy mountains to India's coral strand. It was wedded to words of many a hymn, including Reginald Heber's "From Greenland's Icy Mountains."

Students at Andover Theological Seminary in Massachusetts were singing Smart's tune in 1888 when they requested a poetically inclined classmate, Ernest Shurtleff, to write a graduation song expressly for them.

Ernest Shurtleff was twenty-six years old. He had graduated from Harvard and was making a niche for himself in the literary world when he went to Andover to prepare for the Congregational ministry. Shurtleff wrote the song for the students to sing as they marched

in a body to the ceremony where they would receive their diplomas. And the music he "borrowed" for his poem was "Lancashire," which Henry Smart had composed fifty-three years earlier.

After serving churches in California, Minnesota, and Massachusetts, Dr. Shurtleff went to Germany and established the American church at Frankfurt. He won fame for his relief activities during World War I. He died in Paris in 1917.

When Henry Smart died in 1879, at the age of sixty-six, he was recognized as one of the greatest composers and conductors in England. He had reached his goal, but he had paid a terrible price. Driving himself relentlessly, he went totally blind at the age of fifty-two and for fourteen years dictated his compositions to his daughter. But, like Ernest Shurtleff, Henry Smart is remembered best for a contribution he made to sacred music while a very young man.

> Lead on, O King Eternal,
>   The day of march has come;
> Henceforth in fields of conquest
>   Thy tents shall be our home:
> Through days of preparation
>   Thy grace has made us strong,
> And now, O King Eternal,
>   We lift our battle song.

84. A Composer Lives Through Five Wars

George Coles Stebbins was two years old when General Winfield Scott's army marched out of Mexico singing "Bonnie

Barbara Allen." Twelve years later young Stebbins left his father's farm in northwestern New York State to attend a "singing school" and begin the longest career on record for the writing of music, either religious or secular.

George Stebbins was in his teens when soldiers of the Union Army marched to strains of "The Battle Hymn of the Republic." At twenty-three he was selling songbooks in a Chicago music store and directing music at the Windy City's First Baptist Church. At twenty-eight he was directing the choir at Tremont Temple in Boston when he met evangelist Dwight L. Moody and began singing for revival campaigns. In New Haven in 1878 he took time out from his singing engagements to compose music for Frances Havergal's "True-Hearted, Whole-Hearted." That same year he was singing at Providence, Rhode Island, when he composed music for "I've Found a Friend, O Such a Friend."

In the spring of 1890 Dr. Stebbins chanced to read a poem that was to inspire the composition of one of his most popular hymn tunes. The poem had been written eight years earlier by wealthy Englishman William Dunn Longstaff after hearing a sermon on the text, "Be ye holy; for I am holy."

In the autumn of 1890 Stebbins was leading music in India for Dr. George Pentecost when someone mentioned the subject of holiness. Remembering the poem by Longstaff, Stebbins searched it out from among papers he had saved. He set the stanzas to music. Thus in far-off India "Take Time to Be Holy" was started around the world.

Fanny Crosby referred to George Stebbins as "Dear, sweet Mr. Stebbins." And it was George Coles Stebbins who set many of the blind writer's hymn-poems to music, among them "Saved by Grace" and the popular "Jesus Is Tenderly Calling."

The Spanish-American War was history in 1907 when George Stebbins wrote music for Adelaide Pollard's "Have Thine Own Way, Lord." And while a war-drunken world sang George M. Cohan's

"Over There" during World War I, George Stebbins was still at work at his organ composing music for the church. Then came the "roaring twenties," the depression of the thirties, and Pearl Harbor. Living far up in the Catskills of his native New York state, George Coles Stebbins was an old man.

George Stebbins came in with a war and went out with a war. He saw three wars between. He heard a troubled and torn world sing its songs of battle. But George Coles Stebbins wrote only songs to help men find a better way. From his pen came hundreds of hymn tunes —some of them the most inspiring in the books. When he died, October 6, 1945, he lacked just four months of being one hundred years old. His music has made immortal many a hymn-poem—like this one that speaks the very sentiment for which George Coles Stebbins gave nearly ninety years of his long life.

> Take time to be holy, speak oft with thy Lord;
>   Abide in Him always, and feed on His Word.
> Make friends of God's children, help those who are weak;
>   Forgetting in nothing His blessing to seek.

85. Gospel Songs Still Popular After Almost a Century

The United States was observing its one hundredth anniversary when a type of sacred song lighter than the gospel hymn dawned on the religious horizon and rose to full light. These lilting compositions, identified as "gospel songs," immediately became popular at camp meetings and revivals. They swept the country from

coast to coast. They echoed across the Atlantic. Some literary critics looked down their noses at the lyrics. More serious composers frowned at the music, as did many at the works of Stephen Foster, whose folk songs are said to have started the trend. Nevertheless, the gospel song has become as much a part of America as has Stephen Foster's simple yet immortal melodies. And it is interesting to note that few hymns, in the strict sense, have been written during the present century while the writing of gospel songs still flourishes.

It is interesting also to note the number of gospel song writers that are identified with Ohio and Pennsylvania. To mention but a few from the Buckeye State: "The Old Rugged Cross" is from the pen of Youngstown's Salvation Army worker George Bernard. Cincinnati's William Howard Doane set to music "Rescue the Perishing," "Safe in the Arms of Jesus," and "Pass Me Not, O Gentle Saviour." East Liverpool's Will Thompson wrote "Jesus Is All the World to Me" and "Softly and Tenderly." While the works of these composers are sometimes classified as gospel hymns instead of gospel songs, there is no question about Stark County Ohio's E. O. Excell's lilting music to "Count Your Blessings."

Philadelphia's "singing Irishman" William Kirkpatrick wrote both words and music for "Lord, I'm Coming Home" and composed the tune for "Jesus Saves." The popular Philip Bliss was from Pennsylvania, as was evangelist Dwight L. Moody's famous song leader Ira David Sankey. And when "the lamented Bliss" died in a railroad wreck in Ohio, another Pennsylvanian named James McGranahan took his place with evangelist D. W. Whittle and became to Whittle what Sankey was to Moody.

Though Moody was the more famous, Whittle was the more versatile of the two noted evangelists. D. W. Whittle not only preached the gospel but, under the pen name "El Nathan," also wrote gospel songs for his singer McGranahan to set to music.

Perhaps the gospel songs present a target for both the literary and music critic. But for almost a century these lighter sacred songs have served a useful purpose, and many have found a place in some of the most scholarly hymnals. Such a universal favorite is given below. The words are by evangelist D. W. Whittle under the name "El Nathan." The tune by James McGranahan is familiar to Protestant churchgoers around the world.

142

There shall be showers of blessing:
This is the promise of love;
There shall be seasons refreshing,
Sent from the Saviour above.

REFRAIN:
Showers of blessing,
Showers of blessing we need:
Mercy-drops round us are falling,
But for the showers we plead.

86. A Father Inspires His Son

The elder Johnson Oatman had a rich, powerful
voice. To the people of the town of Lumberton, New Jersey, their
local merchant was the best singer in the state. That's why Johnson
Oatman, Jr., always sat next to his father in church. That's why, as
a small boy, he stood on the pew and looked on the same book with
his father. He loved church music, and he loved to hear his father
sing. Perhaps that's why Johnson Oatman, Jr., grew into manhood
with a fervent desire to contribute something to the faith of his
father.

As a junior member in the firm of Johnson Oatman & Son, young
Oatman found little outlet for his religious ambitions. So he studied
for the ministry and was ordained. But the limits of one Methodist
church narrowed his horizon. He went from one pulpit to another
as a "local preacher." Still he was not content.

Johnson Oatman was thirty-six years old when he found his talent.
If he could not sing like his father, he could write songs for others
to sing. He had found a medium with no limits. He could reach
millions through his sermons in song.

It was in 1892 that Oatman took up his pen. In three years the
world was singing hundreds of his songs, and among them was the
favorite, "There's not a friend like the lowly Jesus, no not one, no

not one . . ." In 1898 presses rolled off a number that is found in hymnals around the world.

> I'm pressing on the upward way,
>> New heights I'm gaining ev'ry day;
>> Still praying as I onward bound,
>> "Lord, plant my feet on higher ground."

It was in 1897 that Johnson Oatman wrote what has been regarded as his most popular gospel song. Composer E. O. Excell, of Stark County, Ohio, set "Count Your Blessings" to music. Of this popular gospel song evangelist Gypsy Smith once said, "Men sing it, boys whistle it, and women rock their babies to sleep to the tune."

Johnson Oatman wrote an average of two hundred gospel songs a year for more than a quarter of a century. His total output passed the five thousand mark. And when publishers insisted, for business reasons, that he set a price on his work, Oatman stipulated his terms. He would accept one dollar per song.

Johnson Oatman was never a great singer. He was never a great preacher insofar as pulpit messages are concerned. But he found his talent, and he made his contribution to the faith of his father. For through his sermons in song he has preached to millions that he could never have reached from the pulpit. He died at Mount Pleasant, New Jersey, in 1926. His messages still reach multitudes through such gospel songs as this one, which he wrote in 1897.

> When upon life's billows you are tempest tossed,
>> When you are discouraged, thinking all is lost,
>> Count your many blessings, name them one by one,
>> And it will surprise you what the Lord hath done.

> REFRAIN:
> Count your blessings,
>> Name them one by one:

144

Count your blessings,
  See what God hath done;
Count your blessings,
  Name them one by one;
Count your many blessings,
  See what God hath done.

87. A Minister Consoles a Grief-stricken Woman

The distraught woman wrung her hands. She was burdened with seemingly unbearable sorrow. Repeatedly she cried, "What shall I do? What shall I do?"

A sympathetic minister replied, "You can do nothing better than tell your sorrows to Jesus." This was the setting for the writing of one of the best known of all gospel songs.

When Pennsylvania's Rev. Elisha A. Hoffman was not working on sermons and hymns in his study, he could be found working among the poor and downcast in the homes of the pastorates he served. By standards of large churches the gentle-mannered Evangelical minister was not a great preacher. By standards of a useful life Elisha Hoffman was, like his father, a great minister.

It was while serving a church at Lebanon, Pennsylvania, some thirty miles from the town of Orwigsburg, where he was born in 1839, that Mr. Hoffman had an experience that inspired the writing of one of his most popular gospel songs. It was while visiting a home where "God had permitted many visitations of sorrow and affliction" that the minister found the woman of the house in the depths of despair.

Mr. Hoffman prayed with the distraught woman, and, as he has it, "I quoted from the Word such passages as 'Come unto me all ye that labour and are heavy laden and I will give you rest.'" Still the woman frantically wrung her hands and repeatedly cried, "What shall I do? What shall I do?" It was then that Hoffman suggested that she could do nothing better than "tell your sorrows to Jesus."

Giving an account of the experience, Mr. Hoffman said that as he left the home the woman "seemed absorbed in her thoughts. Her eyes lighted up, and with animation she exclaimed, 'Yes, I must tell Jesus . . . I must tell Jesus!'" The minister further said that as he left the home he had a "vision of a joy-illumined face . . . and I heard all along my pathway the echo, 'I must tell Jesus . . . I must tell Jesus.'"

Reaching his study, Mr. Hoffman "penned off" the words for one of his best songs. And "before very long" he had composed a melody to suit the words.

Elisha Hoffman was a writer of music as well as lyrics. He wrote music for the verse of other writers. He wrote verse for compositions of other musicians. And quite often he wrote both words and music. Hoffman collaborated with Rev. John Hart Stockton on the old camp meeting favorite "Glory to His Name." It was Mr. Hoffman who wrote the words of "Leaning on the Everlasting Arms" for composer A. J. Showalter. He wrote both words and music for "Are You Washed in the Blood?" Hymns, gospel hymns, and gospel songs came from his prolific pen. But one of his best known is the gospel song that came after his visit to the home of a distraught woman.

I must tell Jesus all of my trials;
  I cannot bear my burdens alone;
In my distress He kindly will help me;
  He ever loves and cares for His own.

REFRAIN:
I must tell Jesus! I must tell Jesus!
  I cannot bear my burdens alone;
I must tell Jesus! I must tell Jesus!
Jesus can help me, Jesus alone.

88. A Great Preacher Pays Tribute to a Great Composer

A Cleveland music dealer offered the young composer twenty-five dollars for four songs. But Will Lamartine Thompson thought they were worth more. He rolled up his manuscripts and returned to his home in East Liverpool, Ohio.

In New York on business for his merchant father, Will Thompson took his songs to a job printer. He would see to the sales himself. Soon after his compositions "My Home on the Old Ohio" and "Gathering Shells from the Seashore" reached the hands of music dealers, the printer hired extra help, and Will Lamartine Thompson was soon to be known as the "bard of Ohio" and the "millionaire song writer."

Those who knew him say that Will Thompson's gift for writing music and poetry was matched with a fine character of sincerity, simplicity, and righteousness. Will Thompson felt that he owed something to the Lord for his good fortune. He turned his talents to writing only sacred songs. He set up his own firm for publishing hymnbooks. And the Lord continued to smile on Will Thompson. His quartet numbers alone sold two million copies. His gospel songs circled the globe and were translated in Africa and Hawaii.

People in big cities could hear big-name gospel singers. But many rural people could not attend the great revivals. There were no phonographs or radios or television sets. So Will Thompson loaded an upright piano on a two-horse wagon and drove into the country to play and sing his own songs. Among them were "Jesus Is All the World to Me," "There's a Great Day Coming," and one of his greatest, "Lead Me Gently Home, Father."

In December, 1899, Will Thompson left his home in East Liverpool and went to Northfield, Massachusetts, to pay his respects to the dying Dwight L. Moody. Visitors were barred from the sick room, but when the noted evangelist heard someone mention the name of Will Thompson, Moody demanded that his friend be admitted.

Feebly, the great preacher, who had "reduced the population of hell by a million souls," took the hand of the man whose talents were matched with "a fine character of sincerity, simplicity, and righteousness."

Will Lamartine Thompson was born in East Liverpool, Ohio, in 1847. He died there in 1909. He lies at rest on a hill overlooking the winding Ohio, which, as a youth, he made famous in song. But Will Thompson is remembered best for the songs of the church which he wrote because he felt that he owed a debt of gratitude to the Lord for his good fortune.

And while the rural people of Ohio spoke of Will Lamartine Thompson's "fine character of sincerity, simplicity, and righteousness," the tribute paid him by the dying Moody summed up the value of his work. For as the great preacher held feebly to Thompson's hand, he said, "Will, I would have rather written 'Softly and Tenderly Jesus Is Calling' than anything I have been able to do in my whole life."

> Softly and tenderly Jesus is calling,
>   Calling for you and for me;
> See, on the portals He's waiting and watching,
>   Watching for you and for me.
>
> REFRAIN:
> Come home, come home,
>   Ye who are weary come home;
> Earnestly, tenderly, Jesus is calling,
>   Calling, O sinner, come home!

89. A Hymn Is Written to Save One Soul

In 1921 Professor William J. Kirkpatrick was eighty-three years old. All of his life he had been accustomed to working long hours. So one night when he told his wife that a song was running through his mind and he would set it down on paper before retiring, Mrs. Kirkpatrick thought little of it. But when she awoke after midnight and saw the light still burning in the study, she called to him.

Music was born into Irishman William J. Kirkpatrick when he came into the world on the Emerald Isle in 1838. Music was a part of him when he migrated to America as a youth. Music was a part of him when, as a Pennsylvania volunteer, he led a fife band during the War Between the States. And music was in William Kirkpatrick's heart when he died in Philadelphia in 1921.

A religious Irishman, Kirkpatrick devoted most of his life to directing church choirs, playing church organs, and writing church songs. He composed music for his own words. He composed music for lyrics from many another pen. In 1882 he took a poem by Priscilla Owens, set it to music, and started the world to singing "We have heard the joyful sound; Jesus saves! Jesus saves!" The same year he wrote music for Louisa Stead's " 'Tis So Sweet to Trust in Jesus." Three years later he composed the tune for "Where the tree of life is blooming, meet me there."

In 1902 Professor Kirkpatrick was leading music for a camp meeting in rural Pennsylvania when he had reason to question the sincerity of a soloist who had been assigned to assist in the singing. Sermons of the evangelist had failed to move the man. So song leader Kirkpatrick decided on a unique plan. He wrote a song, both words and music, especially for his soloist. At the opening of an evening service he handed it to the man in question and asked that he sing it. The soloist did—and joined others at the altar.

On the night in 1921 when Mrs. Kirkpatrick called to her husband, there was no answer. She found the professor in his study, still sitting in his chair. On the desk were unfinished verses of a song.

The last lines indicated that he had worked rapidly. But, like Rev. Edward Hopper, author of "Jesus, Saviour, Pilot Me," he died with a pencil in his hand.

William J. Kirkpatrick went out of the world as he had come into it—with a song in his heart. Tens of thousands of penitents have gathered at the altar to the singing of his songs, especially this one that he wrote to save the soul of one man.

> I've wandered far away from God,
>   Now I'm coming home;
> The paths of sin too long I've trod,
>   Lord, I'm coming home.
>
> REFRAIN:
> Coming home, coming home,
>   Never more to roam,
> Open wide Thine arms of love,
>   Lord, I'm coming home.

90. A Hymn Is Inspired by a Simple Prayer

Many of the world's best-loved hymns have been written by women. And many of the world's best hymn writers were humble folk whose lives were devoted to the cause of making the world a better place.

Such a hymn writer was Adelaide Pollard. Like her mother, who wrote hymns during the Moody-Sankey era, this remarkable woman spent her entire life in the cause of furthering Christianity. But she wanted no recognition for it. Nobody knows how many hymns she wrote, because she rarely signed them.

Adelaide Pollard was forty-five years old when, in 1907, she visited a prayer meeting where she was inspired to write her most famous hymn. It was a simple phrase from a simple but sincere prayer that impressed her. For in offering her prayer an elderly woman omitted the usual beseeching of the Lord for blessings. "It doesn't matter what you bring into our lives, Lord," the woman prayed. "Just have your own way with us."

As she left the prayer service, "Have thine own way" rang in the mind of Adelaide Pollard. On the way home she shaped verses of a hymn in her mind. Before she retired, she had the poem on paper. Shortly afterward, George Coles Stebbins set the lines to music, and "Have Thine Own Way, Lord" was ready for the Christian world— all because of a simple phrase in a simple prayer.

In mid-December, 1934, a seventy-two-year-old woman quietly bought a ticket at New York's Pennsylvania Railway Station. Then she sat down to watch the milling throngs while she waited for her train for Philadelphia. Traveling was not new to the little woman. As a Bible teacher and Christian worker she had been all over the United States. She had spent several years in England. When she was almost sixty years old, she had gone to Africa to do missionary work. And now, past three score and ten, she was waiting for a train to Philadelphia to fill a speaking engagement.

The caller announced the train for Philadelphia. The throngs milled through the gates, but the quiet little woman was not among them. Unnoticed by the hurrying crowd, she sat where she had been stricken. Perhaps the Great Conductor figured Adelaide Pollard had filled enough engagements. For a week later the author of "Have Thine Own Way, Lord" filled an engagement with God. At Fort Madison in her native state of Iowa friends laid her to rest

Have Thine own way, Lord!
Have Thine own way!

151

Thou art the potter,
I am the clay;
Mold me and make me
After Thy will,
While I am waiting,
Yielded and still.[1]

91. A Famous Clergyman Reads an Article

The Lake Michigan steamer pointed her bow south-by-west toward the docks of Chicago. On board was a forty-four-year-old Presbyterian minister who was destined to become one of the most noted clergymen in America. On board the Lake Michigan steamer that day in 1911 was born one of the best known hymns written during the twentieth century.

William Pierson Merrill was born at Orange, New Jersey, in 1867. He earned degrees at Rutgers College, Union Theological Seminary, and Columbia University. He was ordained at the age of twenty-three and took his first pastorate in 1890 at Philadelphia. After five years in the Quaker City, Dr. Merrill went to the pulpit of Chicago's Sixth Presbyterian Church.

Through the centuries various denominations have given impetus to religious movements—foreign missions, home missions, Christian education, temperance, and many another noble cause. At the turn of the century, and for more than a decade after, Presbyterian churches sponsored a world-wide Brotherhood Movement. Ministers preached, laymen spoke, scribes penned editorials, and assemblies were held to further the Brotherhood Movement wherever Presbyterians were found. That's why Dr. Merrill was on board the Great Lakes steamer in 1911. He was returning to his Chicago pulpit after a tour in the interest of the Brotherhood Movement.

---

[1] Copyright 1907. Renewal 1935. From *The Service Hymnal*, Hope Publishing Company, Chicago. Used by permission.

A short time earlier editor Nolan R. Best, of the periodical *The Continent,* had suggested to Dr. Merrill that there was an urgent need for a brotherhood hymn. Editor Best could have made his suggestion to none more capable of filling the need. For William Pierson Merrill was, in addition to being an authority on hymnology, an accomplished poet and composer of music. But having no particular theme in mind, the versatile clergyman promised only to give the suggestion some thought.

To pass time on the steamer Dr. Merrill fell to reading whatever he found of interest aboard ship. He came across an article by Gerald Stanley Lee entitled "The Church of the Strong Men," and the Presbyterian Church was to have its brotherhood hymn before the steamer tied up at the dock in Chicago. After reading the article, Dr. Merrill wrote, "Suddenly this hymn came up, almost without conscious thought or effort."

And so a church movement, an editor's suggestion, a magazine article, the solitude of a boat voyage—and the world was given a great hymn from the pen of a great minister who, that same year, became pastor of New York's noted Brick Presbyterian Church, where he served continuously until his retirement in 1938.

Dr. Merrill lived to see his hymn circle the globe. In a letter dated in 1952, he wrote that he had heard it sung in India, China, and Japan and added that it had gone into forty different countries. Every year editors request permission to use it in new collections. And before his death in 1954 he graciously granted its reprinting here.

> Rise up, O men of God!
>   Have done with lesser things;
> Give heart and mind and soul and strength
>   To serve the King of kings.[1]

[1] By permission of William Pierson Merrill.

92. A Hymn of Hope Is Born of Despair

Ben McKinney was seven years old when the panic of 1893 swept across the nation. At the age of eight he was plowing with his father and six brothers in cotton fields of Louisiana. When the rain and wind of winter came, he sang hymns at family worship in the McKinney log cabin. In the fields he sang original tunes to familiar hymn-poems which, he said in later life, "just came from my mind and heart."

When Ben McKinney was fourteen, his father sent away to a mail-order house for a pump organ. Once when the youth sang a solo while his sister Carrie played, the elder McKinney beamed, "Ben, you ought to make a good singer some day." Thus began a career in evangelistic singing, composing, and gospel song writing that has not been surpassed in the twentieth century.

Baylus Benjamin McKinney was born at the rural Louisiana community of Heflin on July 22, 1886. He was educated at Mt. Lebanon Academy and at Louisiana College. He attended Southwestern Baptist Theological Seminary at Fort Worth, Texas, and furthered his music studies in Chicago. In 1942 Oklahoma Baptist University awarded him the honorary degree of Doctor of Music. After service in World War I he taught at his alma mater in Fort Worth and for seventeen years was music editor for a songbook publisher in Dallas.

In 1935 he became music editor for the Baptist Sunday School Board in Nashville. Consistent with his full life, he continued to teach music in church schools, write, compose, and lead song services throughout the South and Southwest until, in 1952, he went to the reward of a life well spent.

Like many another prolific composer, Ben McKinney never recorded the total number of hymns and gospel songs he wrote. He

once said he supposed he had written about one thousand. Whatever the total, in the *Baptist Hymnal* he runs close behind the prolific Fanny Crosby, Charles Wesley, and Issac Watts. For writing both words and music, B. B. McKinney tops the list with fifteen selections.

Ben McKinney was forty-seven years old when the depression of the 1930's reached its lowest ebb. All about he saw want and despair. Through his influence the Travis Avenue Baptist Church in Fort Worth, where he was serving as assistant pastor, became a Mecca for those in need. And from his pen during the depth of the depression came both words and music for this hymn of hope:

> Have faith in God when your pathway is lonely,
>   He sees and knows all the way you have trod;
> Never alone are the least of His children;
>   Have faith in God, have faith in God.[1]

93. "I Would Not Hear Him Sing Much Longer"

For years C. R. Moore had directed singing at a little Baptist Church at Draketown, Georgia. But on a Sunday in April, 1914, the familiar old hymns had an added meaning. Moore's son James was home from Mercer University, at Macon, and was to fill the pulpit.

Youthful Rev. James C. Moore looked across the congregation with a heavy heart. He had been away only four years. But familiar faces that were young so short a time ago showed traces of age. His nine brothers and sisters had grown up. His mother's health was breaking.

Most of all, the twenty-six-year-old ministerial student was touched by his father's singing. The elder Moore had been trained by the renowned A. J. Showalter, composer of "Leaning On the

---

[1] Copyright owned by Broadman Press.

Everlasting Arms." He had become known as one of the finest singers in Georgia, but now his voice was breaking.

Recalling the occasion of almost half century ago, the son related, "I felt so sorry for him. His voice broke and he lost the pitch of the tones. I knew I would not hear him sing much longer."

Back in school at Macon, James C. Moore wrote both words and music for a hymn. He wrote under the title, "Dedicated to My Father and Mother." Thus, in the pulpit of a little Baptist church in East Georgia was born the inspiration that would become a well-known hymn to be published in hymnals in Australia and printed as sheet music in Canada. In a survey a few years ago an average of eighteen people in every church congregation interviewed said they had buried loved ones to its comforting strains.

As a boy, I rode the circuits of Alabama with my father. I rode with him to many a brush-arbor revival. It was here that I learned to love and cherish the immortal hymns. After almost half a century of service in the North Alabama Methodist Conference, he retired. But he never quit preaching. He never looked with disfavor upon the old-fashioned custom of shouting, and he smiled on those who sat in the "amen corner." For my father was of the vanishing school of gospel preachers.

On a Sunday during the summer of 1954 I visited a small church where he preached his last sermon. During his message he said, "I love the church. I love its people. And I love the old hymns. To me, 'Rock of Ages' is the greatest. And I love the more recently written 'In the Land Where We'll Never Grow Old.'" From the pulpit he looked directly at me and added, "And when my Lord calls me home to glory, I want those two great hymns sung for me while I cross over the river Jordan."

Less than a month after I last heard him preach, I looked across a bank of roses while the choir softly sang "Rock of Ages" and "Where We'll Never Grow Old."

I have heard of a land on the far-away strand,
   'Tis a beautiful home of the soul;
Built by Jesus on high, there we never shall die,
   'Tis a land where we never grow old.

REFRAIN:
Never grow old, never grow old,
   In a land where we'll never grow old;
Never grow old, never grow old,
   In a land where we'll never grow old.[1]

---

[1] By permission of James C. Moore, Sr.

Index *(Numbers indicate pages on which stories begin.)*